Society Founders

Danielle Ackley-McPhail

Greg Schauer

John L. French

Jean Rabe

Patrick Thomas

Jeff Young

Leona Wisoker

Robert M. Price

C.J. Henderson

James Chambers

The Society for the Preservation of
C.J. Henderson

Edited by

Danielle Ackley-McPhail
and Greg Schauer

eSpec Books
Pennsville, NJ

PUBLISHED BY
eSpec Books LLC
Danielle McPhail, Publisher
PO Box 242,
Pennsville, New Jersey 08070
www.especbooks.com

ISBN: 978-1-942990-00-0
ISBN (ebook): 978-1-942990-04-8

Octopus illustration © Christos Georghiou - Fotolia.com
Octipus © aliaksei_7799 - Fotolia.com

Cover Coloration: Erica Henderson

Copy Editor: Wrenn Simms, KRADitorial INC

Interior Design: Sidhe na Daire Multimedia
www.sidhenadaire.com

Dedication

To Cato Vandrare,
who likes CJ's writing a lot
and took the opportunity we provided
to do something for his legacy.

And to CJ's family, Grace Tin Lo,
Erica Henderson, and Iris Feng.
In CJ's world, everything was
always for them.

Contents

Introduction

ON JULY FOURTH 2014, CHRISTOPHER JAMES (C.J.) Henderson lost his battle with lymphoma. The hole he has left in the lives of his family, friends, and in fandom is quite large. While most of his time was spent writing, driving to events, or sitting at a dealer's table hawking his works, he still found time to cook special meals for his family, run *Call of Cthulhu* games for his daughter's friends and for various groups of fans after hours at conventions. He hung out and chatted whenever he could, whether in the green room at some con, or while crashing on a friend's couch watching classic sci fi or really bad B-movies…the kind so bad they are great.

Like those movies, C.J. Henderson was an icon. A cult classic. A fixture in so many of our lives, ingrained enough that we cannot fathom his not being there. He is remembered for his witty banter, his cantankerous grumbling, being both the butt of his own jokes and the granddaddy of all archetypal hucksters. He freely gave his advice, offered opportunities, and inspired up-and-coming authors and veterans alike. Walk into any convention and say his name and twenty heads or more around you will turn to look for him.

While over the last year it became more difficult for him to write, even in his final days the ideas still kept rolling. This man didn't just dabble at writing, he was a born writer and the joy and passion with which he approached that sacred charge has rubbed off on so many others. In this we are blessed. Not only will his work continue to come out for years to come, but the spirit of it will go on much longer through those he inspired and encouraged.

C.J. is much beloved in fandom and has carved a great swath in the literary world, with works in nearly every genre imaginable, with publishers both great and small. I cannot count the number of novels he has penned or the multitude of stories he has had published, but I can tell you that I have seen with my own eyes the way the fans flocked to his table to claim their copies of the titles they didn't yet have. Whatever C.J. did, he did with passion, determination, and confidence. That speaks to something in all of us.

We can't imagine a world without C.J..

We don't want to imagine a world without C.J..

We *refuse* to imagine a world without C.J..

And yet we must.

Physically he is gone from us, but his legacy lives on. As long as we remember and spread the word, he will remain a part of our world.

This is the reason we have formed the Society for the Preservation of C.J. Henderson. Not just for this book or the campaign that made it possible, but as an ongoing tribute to a man that should not be forgotten.

With love and heartache,

Danielle Ackley-McPhail

right: C.J. Henderson and his wife, Grace Tin Lo, at Kotoricon 2014

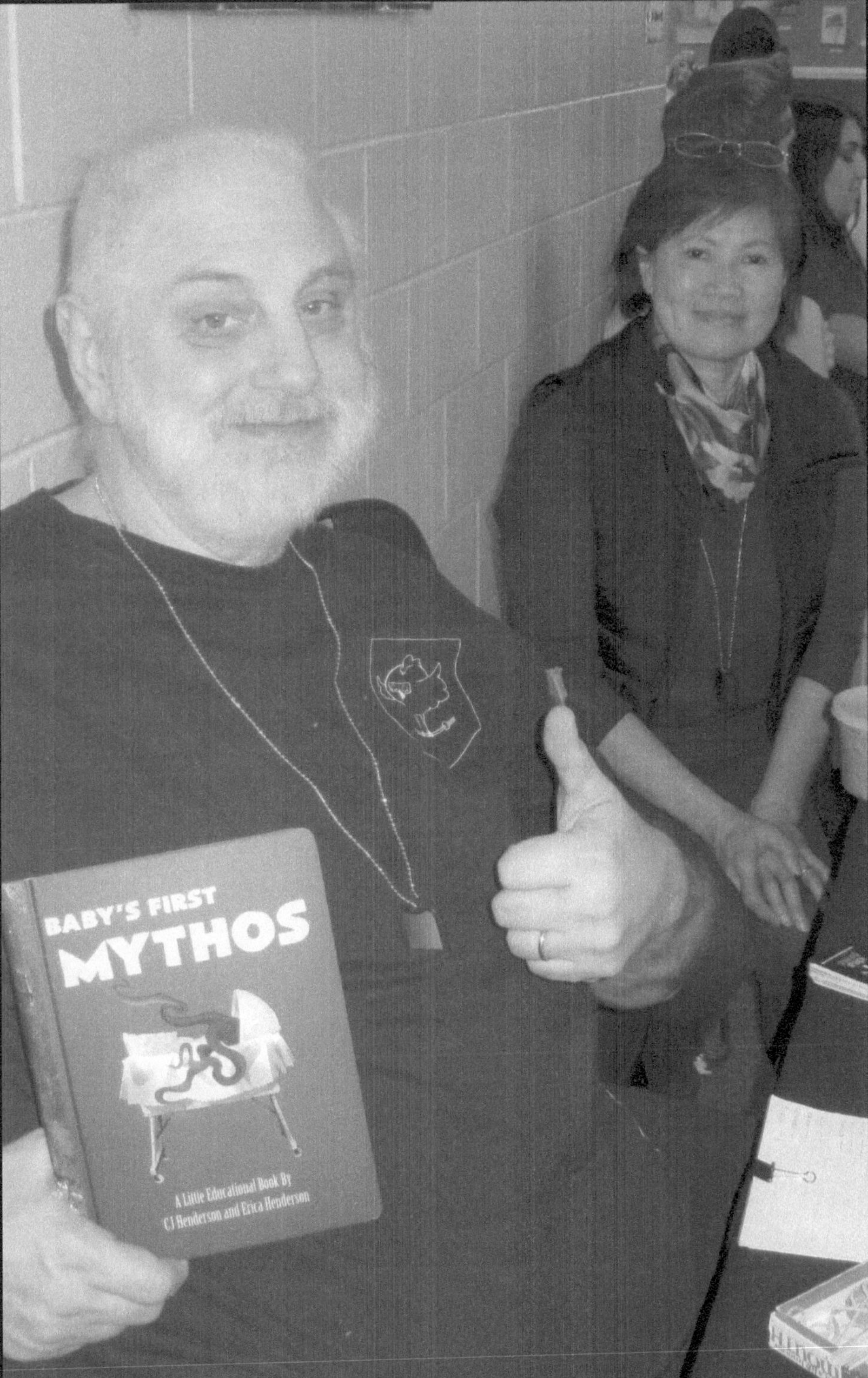

BABY'S FIRST
MYTHOS
A Little Educational Book By
CJ Henderson and Erica Henderson

This story is quintessential C.J., from the characterization of SeeJay himself to the subtle references to both his real-world life and his created worlds. A fitting tribute from one of his closest friends.

The Editors

The idea for my story was the title of the collection: *The Preservation of C. J. Henderson.* I knew right away that it had to be a story in which C. J. himself was somehow protected from something or someone. My first thought was to have in peril at a con. The con somehow became a Renaissance Faire and that quickly changed to a fair held in Medieval Times. And so, C. J. Henderson became Seejay, Son of Hender. As for how the story ties to C. J. Hell, I just opened the C. J. bag and dumped everything out of it and into the story.

John L. French

What Tales He Knows

John L. French

CONOR OF SCOTIA WALKED THROUGH THE FAIR OF Nieves enjoying the dry air and warm weather. Elsewhere storms raged, storms that kept him from boarding a ship and crossing the Norman Sea to Carney, and from there to Caerleon where he hoped to meet brothers-in-arms and perhaps revive an ancient tradition. That the rain and wind had not visited itself on the town and fairgrounds might have been explained by luck. However, the "after storm" smell and a certain tingling in the air told the knight that it was more likely magic at work, magic that guaranteed good weather for the fair at the expense of foul weather elsewhere.

He confirmed this when he sought a room at the Stone Moon Inn. "It's the Wizard's doing," the landlord explained. "Two seasons ago the rains came and washed us all out. No money was to be made that year. And this town depends on what the fair brings in. So does the Wizard, for he gets a share of our earnings. Since then, well, look outside. Even those who don't care to make merry come to Nieves if only to escape the foul mess outside it."

"And the fact that others pay the price for your good weather?"

"What do you think? Look around, my inn is full and I'll make enough to carry me until spring. Yes I know there's no such thing as a free meal, but as long as I don't have to pay for the piper's tune it's all right with me. And even if it wasn't..." the landlord looked in the direction of the Wizard's keep, "…it's all right with *him* and there's naught anyone can do about that."

Conor knew differently. As a wandering knight and sometimes sword-for-hire, he had fought and overcome magic and its users. But he said nothing. It was not his fight. He had stopped at Nieves only because he had to.

"But enough talk about the weather," the landlord said. "What else can I get you? Another ale?"

Conor nodded. "That and a room. From what you tell me I'm here until the fair is over and the weather breaks."

The ale was good and easily poured. The room was somewhat harder to come by. Crowded as the inn was, as all the inns were, Conor settled for a space on the floor of the common room. It was better than sleeping outside, not that it was likely to rain, at least until the week was done.

So with nothing to do and a week to do it in, Conor walked the fair, enjoying what entertainment there was and examining the goods for sale. Most of the latter were from the locals but there were vendors from other parts of the continent as well. A couple from Stratford with what they claimed were fairies in a cage. A brewer from Barrie. Conor was at the stall of a leather smith's trying to decide whether to replace his worn scabbard when he heard;

"Don't walk by. Come, hear the stories. Welcome all to the big, fat, wonderful world of me!"

Conor turned toward the noise. On a makeshift stage he saw a large man in modified jester's garb enticing people to gather round with promises of songs and stories — told and sung for a price of course.

"He's been at that all day," the smith complained. "Every half hour the same rant. It's getting so if he should suddenly go mute, may the saints will it so, I could step in and say it for him."

"But is he any good? Are his tales worth the telling?"

"Who can say? Once the crowd is large enough and there's money in his bowl, his voice drops so that only those who paid can hear him. Now about that hide you hold in your hand. I can fashion you a nice scabbard from in that in no time at…"

But the knight was not listening, his attention now on the storyteller. "Thank you," he told the smith absently. "I'll think about it and be back."

"I've heard that before."

A small group had gathered around the stage, mostly children whose parents had left them while they shopped or sold. The bowl in front of the storyteller was mostly empty, the few coins in it either brass or debased copper.

The minstrel sighed. "For this I could tell a short tale of pirates or dragons."

"Pirates *and* dragons," suggested a young lad in the crowd.

"Would that I could, young sir, but the length of the story depends on the coins in the bowl, and for what I see before me I could only..." he looked out, appealing to what few adults were standing behind the children. No help was forthcoming, but unable to disappoint an audience, no matter its size or age, the storyteller sighed and said, "Perhaps I could tell the tale of Jac and Her Beanstalk."

There were moans and groans and cries of "Not again" and "We've heard that one." And indeed they had, for it had been told twice before and mostly to the same crowd of children.

Conor could wait no longer. "Hold up, Sir Bard," he called and walked up to the stage. Drawing a gold coin from his purse, he dropped in the bowl. "Your finest tale if you would, one of sword, sorcery, and daring deeds. A lengthy tale, one suitable for these fine young people."

Smiling in delight at the coin that shone in the bowl, the storyteller winked and said;

"Many thanks, Sir Knight. What is your name so I can sing your praises at a later time and perhaps add you to a tale or two?"

"I am Conor of Scotia and you do me honor by accepting my coin. In my country, bards and shanachies are revered and it is considered a duty and privilege to support them."

"We are well met, Sir Conor. I am called Seejay, son of Hender and if what you say is true then when this fair is over I may travel with you, if you will have me."

"Let us talk of that another time, Sir Bard. For now you have young folk waiting for a great tale."

"About that, Sir Conor. While the tale I'm about to tell is complete in itself, it would be even better with song. For another coin…"

Laughing, Conor added silver to the gold then sat with the children to enjoy the tale of Princess Eliza and the Dragon Lord. The Bard even made sure to include a few pirates. And in no time at all Seejay had his audience laughing, crying, and singing along.

The noise of enjoyment from the small crowd drew a larger one, then one larger still. Within two turns of the glass it seemed that half the fair had gathered around Seejay's stage where he talked, sang, told jokes, and danced like a monkey whenever a small coin was added to the now-overflowing bowl.

Enjoying himself more than he had since leaving his native land, Conor sat through tales of Jacques of The Hague and London Teddy before deciding to see the rest of the fair. Thanks to Seejay, there were fewer buyers around the other vendors and so Conor was able to bargain for better prices on food, drink, and some of goods he would need for his journey. A man of his word, he did return to the pleasantly surprised leather smith and commissioned a new scabbard to be delivered at fair's end.

Night came, the fair closed. While most vendors were closing their booths and covering their wares, Conor heard;

"Sir Conor."

Turning he saw the storyteller walking toward him. "Master Seejay, was it a good day for you?"

"One of the best, though it could always be better. Still, I am weighed down by the coin that came my way. Could I perhaps trouble you to escort me? I hear there are thieves about, and I speak not just of some of the vendors."

"Again, it is my honor. And as a bard stands higher than a simple knight, call me Conor."

"And I am to one and all simply Seejay."

"Where are you staying?"

The bard at least had the grace to look sheepish before saying;

"The thing is, I failed to make arrangements for proper lodging. Perhaps I could share yours? I'll take up as little room as possible and I do not snore, at least, I have never heard myself doing so."

Again the knight laughed. "You can share whatever part of the floor the landlord has allotted me."

"The floor? Not even a couch?"

"The floor it is. Of course, your golden tongue can probably talk the landlord out of his own bed and into leaving his wife behind."

Seejay smiled at the challenge. "I might at that. A bed would be nice, but as for the wife, tonight I am too tired."

As Conor had expected, the Inn of the Stone Moon was already crowded. Ale and wine flowed and the exhausted barmaids grew tired of serving drinks and dodging the drinkers.

Catching the landlord's eye, Conor told him of the great honor that had been bestowed upon his establishment. The famed storyteller, the most celebrated bard of the continent, the very talk of the Nieves's Fair, had deigned to visit his inn, and for the small price of a comfortable place to sleep and enough mead and ale to keep his throat wet, he would entertain his guests and keep them eating and drinking until the watch ordered the inn closed. When the landlord hesitated, Conor added;

"Or Seejay Hender's son can go elsewhere, but I cannot guarantee that he will not draw your patrons away with him. As I am staying here it would pain me to have to eat and drink alone."

The landlord quickly agreed to the knight's terms. On hearing what Conor had done, Seejay was, for once, speechless. Once he found his voice, his only words were "How?"

"You are a bard, I took training with them. I can tell a tale when I must."

"And a pretty tale it was. Now let us eat and drink before," Seejay looked at the crowd, "I must get to work." He sighed, as if being the center of attention was a great burden to him.

After he had eaten, Seejay began earning his keep by singing a few songs. His rendition of "Stab Them in the Back" soon had most of the crowd, especially what guardsmen were present, singing along. He then told a tale about two men who journeyed to the moon in a giant saucer, until finally he said;

"More later. My throat is dry and demands ale. But while I satisfy my thirst, I present to you a young knight, one trained not only by the feared Red Branch itself but by the very bards of Scotia. He will tell you stories of his great deeds."

Unlike Seejay, Conor did not like to be noticed. He would have demurred, but as a knight he was trained to meet all challenges. So while the storyteller ate and drank, Conor told of a genie who betrayed his master and was then bested by one more clever than he. He followed this with a tale of the merfolk and how a near war between land and sea was narrowly averted. While speaking, he noticed that Seejay listened intently, no doubt making mental notes of the knight's stories so as to add them to his repertoire. Conor ended with a bawdy song about a mermaid and a tortoise before nodding to Seejay that it was again his turn.

"Well," began the storyteller, "as my friend and companion has told a tale of the sea and sang a song about a *tail* of the sea," he waited while those who got the jest laughed, "allow me to continue the theme. Has anyone here present heard of the Deep Ones?"

Conor had, as part of his knightly training. In his travels he had heard them spoken of in whispers and rumors. Conor looked around. Everyone else shook their heads; all save two guardsmen who began listening intently. Seejay spoke of the fish-like creatures that lured men to destruction with promises of gold and power.

The bard's story ended with the navy of the Doge of Venice using Greek Fire to eliminate a town that had been overrun by the creatures. On seeing his audience's fascination with such horrors he began telling of the Old Ones, beings forgotten by creation, cast out of existence, and now lurking on the other side of the world's threshold, waiting to again enter and devour all.

Seejay was speaking of a Sleeper whose awakening would mean the end of all when one of the guardsmen nodded to another. The one who nodded then left but not before saying something to his fellow. Although Conor could not hear what was said by their actions he imagined it was something like "Watch him. I'll bring the others." The knight hoped he was wrong but loosened his sword in its scabbard just in case.

A turn of the glass and Seejay was still speaking. Conor was only partly listening, instead alternately watching the remaining guardsman and the inn door, waiting for something to happen. From what little the knight heard the bard's story was one of fairies and cockroaches.

"Enough for now," the storyteller announced, "for I need my rest if I am to thrill the fairgoers tomorrow with tales of daring deeds."

"One more," shouted several members of his audience.

"I don't know…"

A coin hit the floor near Seejay, then several others.

"Well, if you insist. In the opening days of the Trojan War, an ominous tome falls into the hands of the Trojan High Command. Can our heroes …."

"Seejay, son of Hender …" interrupted a voice from the doorway.

Damn, thought Conor as what was clearly a lieutenant of the guards stepped into the inn. Several guardsmen followed. The one who had remained behind moved to join them.

"Seejay, son of Hender," the lieutenant said again.

"Do you mind? I'm in the middle of a story. If there's a tale you wish told, then come to the fair tomorrow and drop a coin in my bowl."

"You will come with us," the lieutenant said as if the storyteller had not spoken.

Damn, the knight again thought, then stood. "Where are you taking him and by whose authority?" he demanded of the lieutenant.

"What business is it of yours?"

"This man, this noble bard, this honored storyteller, is under my protection."

By now the crowd that had gathered around Seejay to hear his tales dispersed as best they could. Some went upstairs, others hid under the tables, most hugged the walls.

"And who are you and why should I care?"

"I am Conor, a knight of Scotia, son of Seamus, son of Liam, son of Conor and you should care because I will not permit this man to be taken where he does not wish to go." Turning to Seejay, Conor asked;

"Do you wish to go with them?"

Seejay shook his head. "It has been my experience that going with guardsmen in the middle of the night seldom leads to pleasant consequences. I would just as soon stay with you."

"It matters not what either of you wish. The Wizard Maldon demands this man's presence in his Keep."

"Seejay?"

"I would still rather not."

"Behind me then."

"Sir," Conor said to the lieutenant. "Please tell your master that Bard Seejay will await his pleasure tomorrow on the fairgrounds. If it is a story he wants, the bard will tell it gratis, in thanks to the Wizard for hosting the fair in such pleasant weather. Anything else can be discussed at that time."

The lieutenant shook his head. "That, Sir Knight, is not an option."

Conor's hand went to his sword. "Then blood must be spilt."

With Seejay safely behind him in a corner, Conor positioned himself so that the guardsmen could come at him only singly or in pairs. He tried not to kill, recognizing that his foes of the evening were simply men doing their job. He wounded when he could but there were those who fell never to rise again. Slowly he reduced his enemy. A dozen became nine, then six, then three until there was only the one.

"Well fought, Sir Knight," the lieutenant of the guard said. "I told the Wizard that the Guard would be no match for one such as yourself."

"Why fight me then?'

"Because the Wizard ordered me too. Because he needed time."

Conor did not ask "time for what?" As soon as the lieutenant spoke he knew that he had been duped, that the men he fought, the ones he had injured or killed, had been sent merely as a distraction. Behind him came a rumble, then the sound of air rushing through a hole. Conor did not have to turn around to know that Seejay was gone.

Anger almost took the knight. He nearly struck out with his sword to remove the lieutenant's head from his shoulders. But his training held. Anger in battle only got one killed.

"You have until daybreak to leave Nieves," the lieutenant told him. "Accept your defeat gracefully, Sir Conor, and move on. You did your best, but there is now nothing you can do to save your friend."

"I will give *you* until daybreak," Conor calmly replied, "to deliver my message to this Wizard Maldon. He has until to-morrow eve to return the Bard Seejay — unharmed, unspelled, and with a purse twice as heavy as he had when taken."

"Or…"

"Ask your master if he knows exactly of what a Knight of the Red Branch is capable. Our training goes deep. If I must, I will raise armies of the dead. I will call on the spirits of Fairie. I will mort-gage my soul to whatever demon I must to fulfill my vow to one under my protection. Tell your master this. Tell him to return the bard or prepare for war."

Looking into the knight's eyes the lieutenant read truth in what had been said. "I will tell him." He then looked past Conor at his fallen men.

"They will be cared for. Now go."

After the lieutenant left, those remaining gathered around Conor. They all began to talk at once.

"Are you really going to do all those things? Can you?…Will you usurp the Wizard?... You will be killed…You should leave; the storyteller is no doubt already dead…what of the fair?…What of my inn? Who's paying the damages…What about these men?…

With a shout and a wave of his arms Conor silenced them all. "The less you all know the better. Someone fetch a healer for the wounded. Landlord," gold and silver hit a table, "that should be payment enough for what is needed." Looking over the dead,

Conor selected one. Picking up the corpse, he slung it over his shoulder.

"What do you want him for?" asked one of the wounded guardsmen.

Conor looked at the man with cold eyes. "Sometimes an offering is needed. Thank your gods that I do not need a living one." Addressing those remaining he said, "Warn your loved ones. Tomorrow will be a dark day. I go now to summon my forces and prepare for battle. Let none follow or disturb me."

There were moans behind the Wizard Maldon as he asked his Lieutenant of the Guard, "Do you believe him? Can he do all that he said he could?"

The moans gave way to tortured laughter. "Of course he can," said the bound and bloody Seejay. "He's Conor of Scotia, the finest of the Red Branch Knights."

A slight movement of the Maldon's hand caused the bard to groan in pain.

"Silence!" commanded the wizard.

"Very well, if you don't want to know what you're facing."

"You would buy your freedom by betraying your friend?"

More weak laughter came from bound man. "As if you would set me free without learning the secrets you think I have. No, I want you to know all of which Conor is capable, so that you can see what doom awaits you."

Maldon held up his hand, then interrupted the gesture. "Speak, or I will roast the flesh from your leg an inch at a time."

"The man you face has overcome the might of the Jinn. He has plumbed the depths of the sea, defeated the Mer and stolen away their women. He is named for the Hound, who held off Maeve's army single-handed and slew five men after he was dead. He is of the race of McCool and Patricus, who drove demons from the land. He was trained by warriors, priests, and druids. He is one of the most dangerous men on the continent and you have angered him. Release me or suffer. Kill me and you will beg for damnation."

Maldon turned to his lieutenant. "What say you? You took the measure of the man last night."

The lieutenant shrugged. "I know not, my lord. Perhaps. Why else would he take a corpse as an offering?"

"Find him. Stop him!"

"Your pardon, My Lord, but cannot your power seek him out? Last night when you seized the bard…"

"I was seeing through your eyes and I saw your men fail to slay one man, a man who showed no arcane power. Now go, find him before…No wait, there's no need. He has already promised to come to us. Let him raise his armies. Let him call on the Fae. This keep is strong, built to withstand any force. Let them come. Let them surround us. We will wait them out. In the meantime, I will strip this storyteller of all he knows about the Deep Ones and the Old Gods then use their power against my foes."

"As you wish, my lord. I will call my men in to prepare for a siege. But what of the townsfolk? Conor's army may vent its wrath on them."

"What is that to me? You have your orders. Now go."

By nightfall there was not a uniformed soldier in the town. Each and every one had been called to the Keep—the unlucky ones on the outside guarding the approaches. The rest inside, to sell their lives dearly should the enemy force an entrance.

Moans and cries of pain came from the Wizard's chamber. "Again, you damned fool. Tell me what you know of the Old Ones."

Seejay could barely speak. The Wizard had not physically touched him but the bard's eyes were blackened and nearly closed. His limbs ached and he bled from every opening of his body. Spitting out a mixture of phlegm and blood, he whispered painfully. "I have told you what tales I know, as they were told to me."

"You lie." A gesture and Seejay twisted in the chair to which he was bound. "The tomes of which you spoke—*The Necronomicon*, the *Book of Eibon*, *The Ravings of el-Hazred*? How did you come to read them? Where can they be found?"

"Stories, just…made-up stories." Seejay's voice could barely be heard. Blackness approached his mind and whether it was death or unconsciousness he welcomed it.

Maldon paused. He looked through the eyes of the men outside his keep and listened through their ears for signs of battle. There were none. *It is still too early*, he reasoned, *not yet midnight. That is when this knight's power will be greatest. That is the time he will strike.*

"I have had enough of you, storyteller. If you will not tell me what I need to know, your shade will. By the time your friend has marshalled his forces, you will be dead and your bound spirit will have revealed all. But I will give you one chance to earn an easy death. Tell me if you can, to what power would the knight offer a corpse? Of what use to him is a dead man?"

The bard heard the question. It was the only one asked that day to which he truly had an answer. At least, he hoped he did. Then, through what little awareness he had left to him, he heard;

"He was my size."

I know that voice, Seejay thought. He forced his eyes open and saw in the doorway a man in guardsman livery. But this man served no master but himself. It was Conor, and he held a bloody sword.

Without another word Conor stepped forward and swung this sword at Maldon's neck. A gesture of the wizard's hand blocked the swing as if he too held a blade. Another gesture and pain shot through the knight's body.

Conor, however, was not a storyteller. He was a warrior and he had felt pain before. He had been trained to ignore it, to shunt it into a part of his mind not concerned with the battle and worry later about any damage.

"Fight the man, not the weapon," his teachers had told him and so he did, striking again at the wizard. Again Maldon parried, but this time Conor was ready with a riposte, blocking the force of the wizard's blow with his blade.

It was strange sort of duel, a man with a sword against one without yet both equally armed. The wizard had not been trained to fight, with the power from his hands he had not needed to — until he faced Conor. But that power was enough to hold off the knight who had to defend against more than simple blades. He had

the skill to do so, but not the time. Soon real guardsmen would enter. If he turned to face them Maldon would strike him down. If he did not, the guardsmen would.

Conor fought on, waiting for his chance, looking for an opening, listening for the sounds from the hall that would mean his end. He decided to risk all on a single rush, hoping he could endure the pain long enough to thrust his sword through Maldon's chest and that such a blow would kill the wizard. He readied himself then…

"The Fae! They rise! They come!" came a weak but audible cry from the man bound to a chair.

For a second, maybe less, Maldon was distracted; his eyes flickering around the room. It was a second too long. In a fight to the death, less than a second is a lifetime. Conor's blade pierced the wizard's heart, then withdrew and cut deep into his neck. Maldon fell. With a downswing Conor made sure he would not rise again.

As Maldon's head rolled free his spells died. The storm ceased to ignore Nieves and hard rain fell.

Conor was cutting Seejay free when the lieutenant of the guard came into the chamber.

"Maldon's dead," the officer said, seeing the body on the floor.

"Yes, he is," Conor replied, his sword at the ready. "Have you a problem with that?"

The lieutenant thought back to his last exchange with Maldon. "What is that to me?" the wizard had asked when advised of possible harm to the town. "No, my duty is to Nieves."

"Then you best be about it, Lieutenant. The storm outside is bad and getting worse. You and your men will be needed."

The officer nodded and turned to leave but before he did;

"There wasn't any army of the dead or from Fairie, was there?"

Conor shook his head. "Just another story, Lieutenant."

"One you both told well."

Conor looked at the now-freed Seejay. Smiling as best he could, the bard said, "I surmised your plan and improvised." Wincing as he stood, he added, "And it's a good thing I did or you might not have beaten him. What would you do without me?"

"Without you I would be in a nice warm inn with a tankard in one hand and a comely wench on my knee. Now I'm bloody, battered, and bruised and likely to be drenched when I leave this place."

"At least the rain will wash away the blood." Looking down at the wizard's body, the bard said, "Damned fool. I tried to tell him, I'm just a storyteller, telling what tales I know."

"You are more than that, Seejay, son of Hender. You are a mighty bard, one who helped defeat a powerful wizard then faced a terrible storm."

The bard thought for a moment. "That's not bad, if I do say so myself."

"Don't worry, Seejay, sooner or later, you will."

Having had these types of conversations with C.J. and knowing how he loved movies of absolutely every type we know he would have loved this story for its simplicity and its subtlety.

The Editors

CJ and I used to throw old movie titles back and forth. I'd say: "With Six You Get Egg Roll," and he'd say: "If It's Tuesday, It Must Be Belgium."

So...for a giggle...I have a talking gun in a Shadowrun novel I'm writing. My PI says something about the killer's victim number six. The gun says. "Six. With Six You Get Egg Roll." No one will get it, but it made me smile.

This story is a tribute to those conversations with my dear friend.

Jean Rabe

Star Lights

Jean Rabe

LONDON KNEW HIS MISSOURI FOX TROTTER WAS out of place in the rugged hills of the southern Nevada Territory. Hell, he thought he was out of place, too, ought to be writing adventure stories to send to them New York magazines. Had two published last year. Just needed to get him some more ideas. In the meantime maybe he ought to be working for a cattle baron rather than following the old man out into the damnable desert on account of they'd seen star lights come to ground last night.

London was working as a hand for the old man—Nathaniel Smith—just until Smith's son came back from a trip out east. But he wished he hadn't accepted the offer for work, had moved on to California and its rumored cool breezes. That'd be a better place to get ideas for stories.

"Sorry I had to bring you out here, Princess." London rubbed the horse's neck, and then swung himself out of the saddle. The horse was nearly sixteen hands high and roan red, with a narrow blaze on her face as white as a newly-painted gospel mill. Her eyes, intelligent and expressive, coupled with half a bottle of Irish whiskey, caused London to part with all his worldly wealth and buy her two years past in Eagle Station.

Most of the money he'd earned doing odd-jobs after that was also spent on her...the finest feed, expert grooming when he rode into a reasonable size town, the most expensive saddle he saw when he was in Cheyenne; it had rounded streamlined skirts and three-point rigging, a full and comfortable seat, and a roping horn that was wrapped with red-latigo. The stirrups were leather-covered too.

London led her under a rocky outcropping where the shadows would grow longer as the morning progressed. He tugged a wooden bowl from her saddlebag and filled it to the brim from a large canteen. Then he tied her to a metal spike he'd driven into the rock on the last trip here, making sure she wouldn't get loose and yet could reach the water. He couldn't bear to lose this horse, which he considered his closest friend.

"I won't be gone too long, Princess." He gestured toward the entrance of a mine a dozen yards away, then wiped at the sweat beading thick on his craggy face. "It's already as hot as a whorehouse on nickel night, and I reckon it'll only get worse. Old Nate here, he doesn't take this heat none too well either. And I don't need to keep you out in it too long and...."

"Quit jawin' to that damn crowbait and get a wiggle on!" Nathaniel pulled off his shirt. He folded it and set it at the mine entrance with a rock on it to keep it from blowing away in the event a wind kicked up. His ribs gleamed with sweat, and London swore the old man was so lean that if he didn't start eating more his bones were going to burst through his shoe leather-colored skin.

"I'll be along directly, Nate. Have to finish seeing to Princess first." He stroked the horse's mane.

"Damn crowbait, that horse is."

London gathered his face into a point, and then his expression softened when he scratched at a spot between the horse's eyes. "Now don't you be insulting her, Nathaniel Smith. Princess is a far piece better'n what you ride. An' I bet she's smarter than both o' us put together."

Nathaniel snorted. The old man hadn't tethered his swaybacked packhorse to anything, expecting—as usual, London figured—for it to be waiting for him when he was finished.

"Get a wiggle on, I say again, Teddy! I'll be as ornery as a fried toad if I have to wait another minute for you! I ain't payin' you to talk to that big horse." The old man was studying the dirt around the mine entrance, one hand on the revolver holstered on his hip. On the way here London had watched him; Nate had stopped every few minutes and studied the ground, brow furrowed and lips working the entire time. "Don't see no boot tracks. Some funny marks here, though. And here and here." He pointed to narrow ruts that looked like a heavy snake might leave behind. "I want to be sure no one's claim jumping on me, gettin' gold that tain't theirs."

Last night a granger from Dutch Flats told Nathaniel and London that as he was driving cows past he saw a blue foggy glow coming from high in the hills, and that he heard an odd howling noise: *Wooooohooooooohooooo.*

Nathaniel and London rode out a ways and didn't see the foggy glow, but they did see what looked like a handful of stars dropping down out of the sky, coming to ground right about where Nate's mine was. But Nathaniel didn't cotton to the desert at night, and London figured the star lights had spooked the old man. So Nathaniel decided to investigate the next morning, when there were no stars to be seen.

The old man ordered London along, despite the heat, which was even more oppressive today than usual.

"Maybe we only thought we saw something last night, Nate. Stars can't really drop out of the sky. Though that might make a good adventure story. Them star lights....maybe they was big lightning bugs. And there weren't no foggy blue glow like the cowman claimed. Maybe we were all half seas over, full as a tick." London rested his hand against a beam at the entrance, while he waited for Nate to light a lantern. He stared out away from the mine entrance and across the uncompromising land. On a low hill in the distance stood a large Joshua tree. Closer were clusters of creosote, saltbushes, and yucca, all looking brittle. "Whiskey can make a man see things, you know."

"*You* should well know that, Teddy. Whiskey can make a man spend too much on a red crowbait," Nate growled, pointing to Princess. "And 'sides, I don't care what I saw about dropping stars last night. I care about these marks at the entrance to my mine. I care about thieves. Now bring that other lantern. Maybe there's more tracks inside. Maybe we'll catch us some claim jumpers." Softer: "And maybe I'll shoot 'em right dead."

London reluctantly lit the second lantern and followed the old man, hearing Princess nickering, and then hearing nothing but the *click* and *shush* of his boot heels against rock and stretches of dirt.

"We ain't gonna be down here too long, are we Nate? It's real hot this morning, and you know I don't like to leave Princess...."

"Hobble your lip about that horse, Teddy." The old man stopped and held the lantern close to a patch of dirt. "More of 'em, see? Wigglin' lookin' marks. Just like on the outside. T'weren't here before, these marks. None of 'em, not that I'd seen. These are fresh. My bones may be old, Teddy, but my eyes are in apple pie order. Might be drag marks. Might be they found some gold and drug it out of my mine. Stole from me!" He resumed his pace, the shaft going down at a steeper angle now.

"You been working this mine for what ... three years, you told me? You said you ain't found no gold in it. How's anybody else in these parts gonna find...."

Nate snorted. "There's gold here, all right. Somewhere. I know it. I can feel it." The old man raised his lantern, squinting as he studied a gouge in the stone near the roof of the shaft. It was sharp-edged and deep, looking just like the tracks he'd pointed to outside in the dirt. "This wasn't here before neither, none of these marks."

The air wasn't as dry where the shaft angled to the west and went deeper still. It didn't smell like dust and stone, it smelled like something London couldn't put a name to, and it overpowered the odor of his sweat. It wasn't a pleasant or unpleasant odor, but it hung heavy and settled strongly on London's tongue.

"Princess, she don't like this bad heat, Nate. She's a right pretty horse. How long you think we're gonna...."

"Shut your bazoo!" Nate made a fist with his free hand and waved it. "I think I hear somethin' other than your jaw flappin'."

London cocked his head. "I hear something, too."

It was like whistling, a sound the wind might make whipping through breaks in the hills. But the air remained still, and so no wind could be responsible for it. The sound changed pitch as they stood and listened, coming lower now. Then the ground beneath their feet started vibrating, and stone dust filtered down from the ceiling. London stretched an arm to the nearest beam and felt the wood trembling.

"Maybe we should come back later," London suggested, his voice little more than a whisper. "I'll ride Princess over to Broken-Nose Simpkins' place, get him and his hands to come back here with us."

"Ya got no sand, boy," Nate shot back. His free hand pulled the gun from its holster. "Wish you was heeled."

"Ain't never carried no gun, Nate. Don't think I'd know how to...."

Suddenly light spilled from around the corner, pale blue like the color of fog that wraps around the yucca on early autumn mornings. The light grew brighter, and the whistling louder.

"Th-th-the light the granger said he saw," London stammered. "Foggy blue."

"Probably the same."

"And th-th-the noise he heard."

"Probably the same."

"We should leave, Nate, like I said. Skedaddle back to your ranch and I'll go to Broken-Nose's and get some other fellers to come with us. I'm a might nervous 'bout this. Worse than a cat in a roomful of rockers. Don't know what might be 'round that corner."

"Claim jumpers is what's around that corner, boy. And they's doing something to make this mine tremble like a frightened babe. Doing something to make that foggy blue glow."

"Can't be claim jumpers," London countered. "Ain't no horses outside 'cept ours. Ain't nobody would walk here in this heat. Too far from anywhere. Don't know what might be around that corner, and—"

"I thought you'd be someone to ride the river with, London," Nate growled, as he edged toward the bend, steadying himself against a beam as the ground shook a little harder. "I thought you had sand. That's why I hired you to help me keep things up. That's why—"

"I'm not afraid," London returned, working up some spittle and failing in his attempt to sound brave. "I'm just thinking there might be ghosts down there." He straightened. Ghost? Now that's the stuff of an adventure story. "A ghost. We should go take a look."

"Ghosts?" The word was like a piece of spoiled meat the old man spit out.

"Yeah, that *woooooohooooohoooooo* sound. Ain't natural. Sounds spooky, like ghosts."

Nathaniel drew the hammer back and edged forward, revolver leading. "Tain't no such thing as ghosts, Teddy. But, yeah, we should go take a look. Ghosts. You oughta be writin' fairytales. Tain't no ghosts."

"Nate, some o' them little places up north, they're starting to call them ghost towns."

"This is a mine, London, not a town. And there tain't no ghosts. Just claim jumpers. Bet they got dynamite."

"L-l-look! Th-th-that ain't no claim jumper, Nate!"

Nathaniel had nearly reached the corner when something stepped out to meet him. Small, it had the shape of a man, though it wasn't a man. Its legs and arms were even thinner than the old man's, elbows and knees exaggerated, like its skin was stretched painfully tight over its bones. Its fingers—three of them on each hand—were long and ended in nails that glimmered liquid gold in the odd, blue light; matching nails were on its three toes.

"Them's what made the marks," Nate said, pointing to the thing's feet and fingers. "Tain't no ghost."

"Ain't human," London said too softly for Nate to hear.

The old man did not seem flustered by the creature's appearance. Rather, he appeared angry.

Its head was overlarge for its body, bald with the tiniest of ears. Its eyes glistened saucer-wide, gold, and devoid of pupils. It didn't seem to be wearing clothes, as all over it was shiny, as if it had been dipped in molten silver.

"N-n-nate, I think that there's a demon." London took a step back. "Princess and me should've went to California." He motioned for Nate to follow. But Nate's eyes were narrowed and locked onto the creature. "We gotta get out of here, Nate. I gotta see to Princess." *And I gotta write about this.*

Nate aimed the revolver at the glimmering apparition. It regarded him almost curiously and opened its little mouth. The *wooooohoooooohooooo* sound came out.

"A demon, I say." London took another step back and then another, wiping furiously at the sweat that was running into his eyes. His chest hurt and his throat felt hot and tight. "I got Princess to think about." If something happened to him, who would take care of that beautiful horse? And who would write down the description of the demon for a New York magazine?

Nate fired, the bullet striking the apparition in the chest. Surprise flashed across its smooth face, and its thin silvery fingers clutched at the hole the bullet made. Something dark green spilled out of the wound; and the little man threw back its overlarge head and howled "*Woooooohoooooooohoooo.*"

"Tain't a ghost, London. Ghosts don't bleed. Tain't a demon. No such thing."

"Ain't a man neither, Nate. Men don't bleed green."

The creature dropped to its knees, then pitched forward with a final *woooohoooohoo.*

"See, tain't a demon. Can't kill demons with bullets. Can't be an angel either. No wings."

"Then maybe it's something real special, Nate. See how shiny its skin is? Just like silver from a mine. Its eyes are gold. Maybe it's a mineral man."

"A mineral man? Helluva imagination you got, Teddy," Nate said with a chuckle. "C'mon. Let's see if there's more of 'em." Nate disappeared around the corner.

London rubbed at his chest, looked up the shaft behind him, and then cautiously followed the old man, swallowing the dry lump forming in his throat and grabbing a beam when the ground shook beneath him again. He ought to be able to get a couple of adventure stories out of this, maybe write full time.

The tunnel widened—as did London's eyes. A cavern loomed down and away, the walls smooth and not worked by man or nature, shot through with veins of gold as thick as a fence post. He heard the old man mutter: "See, I told you there was gold. Them funny-looking claim jumpers exposed it for me."

In the center of the cavern was a great glob of metal, the size of a large chuck wagon but looking like an overturned soup bowl. It was that thing casting off the foggy blue glow, and by its vibrations causing the ground to shudder. Above it was open sky—a rent in the hill that London suspected was recent, judging by how jagged and sharp the broken rocks looked. And around the glob of metal a dozen of the silvery men worked, all of them *woooohooohoooo*ing to each other in various tones and loudness.

Then suddenly all of them were looking at Nate and London.

One of them grabbed up an object that resembled an anvil, though it had blinking lights, and strands of something like horsehair protruding from its top.

"Nate, I got me enough material now. I think me and you should skedaddle on out o' here and—"

Nate dropped his lantern and aimed his revolver at the one holding the anvil. "Tain't no mineral men going to cheat me out of my gold, you hear me! I reckon this one—whatever it is—has to be the biggest toad in the puddle. He's taller than the rest. I take him out an' the others might well skedaddle themselves back to wherever they came from. I'll let them see just how formidable I am." He drew out for-mid-eeee-bul and made a smacking sound with his lips.

Then Nate fired twice, the first bullet striking the anvil and sending sparks in all directions. The second caught the silvery creature in the neck and sent it reeling backward, making it drop the device.

The cavern erupted in a cacophony of *woooohoooooohoos*, screeches, and sputtering crackles, the latter coming from the anvil, which continued to spark, and which now had started to glow red-hot. The silvery men waved their spindly little arms and ran—some of them toward their downed fellow, some behind the overturned soup bowl, three toward Nate.

The old man took aim and fired one bullet into each of the three figures charging him. He hit two in the chest, the third in the center of its face. All of them fell and *woooohooohooo*ed in hurtful high-pitched tones that caused London to drop his lantern and clamp his hands over his ears.

The anvil glowed brighter and the sparks came wilder. The silvery men ran away from the sparking contraption now and disappeared into the overturned soup bowl, which glowed ever harsher. The ground shook more fiercely, and London fell, unable to keep his balance.

"Princess," he whispered. "Dear God, let Princess be all right."

Nate reloaded and fired at the soup bowl, the bullets bouncing off the metal. Then he, too, fell—as the cavern bucked and rocked, and cracks split open in the floor. The anvil burst into a shower of ruby-colored stars and then roared like a maddened beast, erupting in flames that whooshed toward Nate and London.

"Princess!" London hollered. "I gotta get to—"

The smallish guide rode a roan red Missouri Fox Trotter, a real show horse. He patted her neck, slid from her saddle, a fine leather one with rounded streamlined skirts and three-point rigging, a full and comfortable seat, and a roping horn that was wrapped with red-latigo. The stirrups were leather-covered too, all of it oiled and well-cared for. The guide waited for his tour group to get off their rented horses.

"See that slash in the rocks?" His gloved hand pointed to the entrance of what had been Nate's mine. A bleached-white horse skull had been nailed above it. "That's one of a half-dozen haunted mines in this area. Played out close to a hundred years ago by prospectors looking for gold and finding nothing but death, the hills so unstable their tunnels collapsed on them. They say on still nights if you go close to the entrance of this particular mine you can hear the spirit of a broken-down swayback softly nickering, and the cry of an owl—*woooohooohoo*. A few have claimed to hear the cackle of an old man and the sounds of gunfire."

"Do you believe in all of that nonsense, Mr. London?" This came from a middle-aged woman wearing an Astros baseball cap and a sweat-soaked "I Escaped from Area 51" T-shirt.

"Ain't no such thing as ghosts," said her companion. "Now let's get done with this and visit those alien landing sites."

"Do you believe in them?" she persisted to the tour guide. "Ghosts? Aliens?"

The guide smiled and nodded. He sweated fiercely under the full-face mask he wore—the one he had specially made in the image of a writer he'd met decades past. "There are lots of spirits and long-lived odd-such things in Nevada, ma'am." Much softer: "Stranded, long-lived things that can extend the lives of beautiful Missouri Fox Trotters." He ran his fingers through his horse's mane, and she wuffled in pleasure. At his wrist, a little silvery skin showed between the glove and end of his shirt sleeve. "C'mon, Princess, we've got more ground to cover with these fine folks before lunch.

There is nothing we could add to the truth and wisdom below. C.J. was a great man and author who did not believe in his own greatness.

The Editors

C.J. was my friend. Over the years we'd talked about all manner of things. It might surprise some to find out he sometimes described himself as a big softie. He could get teary eyed when telling a story, whether his or another than touched him. One in particular that turned him into a big softie was the finale of his Rocky and Noodles stories.

Like many of us who call ourselves writers, C.J. was a dichotomy. On one level C.J. knew he had the talent and skill to make a story sing, while on another he was often surprised and even taken aback after talking to someone his work truly touched.

C.J. knew the end was coming. His big concern was for his family who were always his first and last priority. Like all who cared for him, I wanted to change C.J.'s fate, but that was beyond me. Beyond any of us. I wanted C.J. to know what he meant to people. A lot of people did and many let him know in different ways, which much like unexpected praise for his writing, astounded him and touched his heart. Besides just telling him, I wanted to do something to show him. I came up with two ways. I made a video at a con which was kind enough to have me as GOH. It was a parade of people paying tribute to C.J. by dancing like a monkey for a nickel. C.J. let me know it made him cry. Not once, but twice. The first time while he was in the hospital getting chemo and then again the next day when he played it for his wife, who was the love of his life.

The second was this story. The tale of a world where C.J.'s stories and characters inspired others to stand up and fight the good fight. A story in which the worlds in which he poured his soul, sweat and tears into took on a life of their own in his readers. A world in which C.J. got to come back to help us all.

Some people say there are an infinite number of universes where everything and anything can happen. I like to think that there's at least one where C.J. is still plugging away on an ancient computer with an antiquated word processing program and making even more new worlds.

Patrick Thomas

Henderson Rising

Patrick Thomas

"D{\small O YOU THINK IT COULD REALLY BE HIM AFTER} all these years?" the tiny woman said, playing pack mule under a tremendous amount of electronic equipment.

"We've had so many false finds over the years, I tend to think not," the large man in the suit and Fedora said.

"But you can't ever give up, even when the odds are stacked so high against you that it blocks out the sun. That's what He taught us," the tiny woman said.

"I haven't given up. I'm here, aren't I? The rebels stashed away so many people who were important to the cause, I stopped getting excited every time one of the Henderson clans finds a cryopod. Only one of them was the great one, the creator of the big wide wonderful world of Him. Only one so loved the world that he would dance like a monkey for a nickel to make the masses happy, because He taught us that everything is better with monkeys. It is He whose words we follow, whose writings still inspire us after all these years."

"Say what you will, but I think this one is actually him. After all, it's the first one ever found in Brooklyn, the place where he raised his family," the tiny woman said.

The skinny girl trailed behind them, writing furiously in a notebook.

The noble Henderson clans had banded together once again, united in hope, but in a hurry. Each clan was based on one of the Great One's characters or books. One of the Hagees — those who based their code of honor on the books of hard-boiled private eye Jack Hagee — had collected one of the Wezleskis, scientists who followed the code of the Pelgimbly Institute for Advanced Sciences stories. With luck they would be able to stay one step ahead of the Conformity Police who were hunting all the clans in the hope of destroying them forever.

"Listen scribe, you're drawing attention," the Hagee said.

"I'm just writing. It's my job," the scribe said.

"And my job is to keep you both safe. Nobody writes these days. You'll draw unwanted attention that we don't need. The conformity cops know the clans are on the move. We don't need some bad Samaritan dropping a dime on us and blowing this whole operation or we're all screwed," the Hagee said, then turned to the woman in the lab coat. "I need to get you off the street."

The shadows began to move as if they were trying to get away from the flashing lights of a police car.

"Down here now," the Hagee said. He grabbed some of the scientific equipment and rushed the two women down a set of sunken steps. They lay on the ground until the car went by.

"Think they're after us?" the scribe said.

"Maybe." The man in the hat hustled the women back onto the street.

"Who found this one?" the skinny scribe asked.

"The B&Bs."

"The Blakely and Boles clan are excellent explorers. After all, the originals in *His* books were crypto-zoologists," she said.

"How much time do we have before the CPs find us?" the woman in the lab coat said.

"The Richards are using all their media savvy to redirect them. As far as we can tell the master programmers have no idea we're here."

"Do you think Marv Richards would have been able to use his Challenge of the Unknown Show to stop the rise of conformity if he was real?" the skinny girl asked.

"Don't know. I'm more concerned about not getting caught and losing our freedom or the cryopod. Who's handling security for the site? I know it isn't the Hagees," the man with the hat said.

"It's your job to get us there safe. The Londoners have security."

The Hagee nodded. There was a rivalry between his people and the Londoners, but they were still members of the Henderson clans. Their clans were very similar, both based on PI's, although Teddy London dealt with the supernatural and Jack Hagee more with the seamier, dark side of life.

If asked, he would always say the Hagees would do a better job of anything, but he knew the Londoners were almost as good. Almost.

They came to a brick building. Two men and a woman stood on the street outside. To the casual observer they were just talking, not standing watch. The two groups nodded to each other. The tiny woman playing pack mule and the man in the hat walked inside the building and down into the basement. The other trio followed them in. The scribe looked once behind her, half-convinced she was being followed, but she saw nothing and trailed behind the others.

Inside there was a man dressed in clothes out of the 1800s examining a metal pod that had been hidden behind a wall. The sheetrock in front of it had been smashed away.

"What has the Ministry of Extraordinary Weapons determined?" the tiny woman said. In the safety of the building, the skinny girl took her notebook and pen back out.

In the Great One's works, the Ministry was Great Britain's answer to the worst weapons steampunk could imagine. In the real world, they are the clans' answer to finding forgotten tech like the cryopods.

The Hagee brushed by her.

"This cryopod contains a male with white hair and a white beard," said the man dressed in steampunk style, wiping off his goggles.

"Maybe the rebels hid Santa Claus," the Hagee said.

"The Ministry teamed with the B&Bs once they found it. However, we felt it best to have the finest of the Wezleski's be the one on hand to actually open the cryopod, so we sent for you."

"Good call," the tiny woman said.

"Can you open it?" the Ministry man asked, putting his goggles back on top of his head.

The tiny woman smiled. "This isn't my first rodeo or my first cryopod. I'll get it open. Are the preparations in place once whoever's inside is awake?"

"Yes, we have a Wan standing by."

The scribe continued writing her notes.

Lai Wan was cursed with the ability to sense the history of everything she touched. The Wan's tried to protect others from what the evil of the world showed them.

The scribe watched the scientist work, then once again took pen to paper.

The tiny woman took out electronic pads and connector cables then inserted them into the cryopod. She worked for over an hour without a break, stopping only once to tell everyone else to leave the chamber for their own safety. The cryo gas might leak and any exposure would render them unconscious.

The scribe and the others went upstairs. The man in the hat moved to a window and stared out.

The scribe moved to his side. "What's happening?"

"CPs are pulling a raid down the block. They know we're in the area. We need to get everyone out of here."

The back door was kicked open. The other raid had been a distraction. The man in the hat reached for his gun, but a quintet of red dots from laser sights convinced him to put his hands in the air instead. One of five armored cops frisked him and took his gun. They did the same to the others.

"It's over, deviant. Where's the pod?" asked a man in a suit.

"Go to hell."

The scribe wrote:

The Conformity Cop punched the Hagee in what He would have described as the bread basket.

"You, girl. Drop the pen," the cop said, pointing a gun between her eyes. She obliged. "Before I run you in for violation of the creative writing ban, where is the pod?"

The scribe shook her head.

"Writers are eligible for the death penalty these days. That means I can shoot you and not have to fill out any paperwork."

"Good thing, otherwise that would make you a writer and you'd have to shoot yourself," she said.

The cop flashed a fake smile and smashed the girl across the face with the barrel of his gun. She fell, blood pouring from her mouth.

"Tell me and I'll forgo the execution and just book you," the cop said.

"Downstairs," she spat.

"No!" screamed the man in the hat.

"You two stay and watch these deviants. The rest of you follow me," the cop said, as the armored officers stepped behind him into the basement.

The man in the hat crawled to the scribe. "You betrayed the clans."

"Wrong. The Wezleski was worried about what the cryo gas was going to do to us. When she sees those cops, she'll vent it," she whispered. "That means we need to take out these two out. I'll take the one on the right. You take the one on the left…on three."

"Wait," the man said.

It was too late. The scribe was already counting. "…Three!"

The girl leapt up, bringing her knee up into the CP's groin, beneath the armor. She ripped his helmet off and smashed his head into the wall, knocking him out. The Hagee smashed the other cop in the jaw, breaking it and knocking him to the ground unconscious.

The man in the hat shook his hand in pain.

"You okay?" the scribe asked.

"Probably busted a knuckle. That was some nice work you did there," he said. "You ever decide you don't want to be a scribe, you'd make a great Hagee."

The skinny girl blushed. The man in the hat retrieved his automatic, then took a gun from one of the fallen cops and handed it to the scribe.

A white mist floated up from the downstairs.

"Looks like you were right," he said, turning to the man from the Ministry. "How long until the gas become inert?"

"Five, six minutes," the Ministry man said as some of the others bound the unconscious cops.

The Hagee looked at his watch, then pointed the gun at the open door and waited. At the seven-minute mark, he said, "Let's go."

The representatives of the collected Henderson clans slowly descended the stairs into the basement. Four cops lay unconscious on the floor, but something or someone was moving.

There was a great sigh of relief as they saw the Wezleski wearing a gas mask on her head.

"Are you okay?" the Hagee asked.

The woman in the lab coat nodded and took off the mask.

"It's ready," she said.

"Who gets to open it?" the Ministry man said.

"Him," the small woman said, pointing to the man in the Fedora. "The Jack Hagee stories were his first great works. It seems only appropriate that one of the firstborn clan welcome the Great One back."

"That's if it really is him," the Hagee said.

"Oh, it's him all right. I decoded the electronic lock and it revealed who was inside," the small woman said, holding up the pad. On it was a name—Christopher John "C.J." Henderson.

"Then our hopes have been answered," the Hagee said, reaching down to pull a handle that looked like it belonged on a refrigerator from the 1950s. He pulled the front of the pod open. Inside, the man with the white hair and beard slowly stirred.

When he opened his eyes, he gave a startled yelp at the sight of the dozen people crowded around, staring at him and smiling. "Where am I? When am I?"

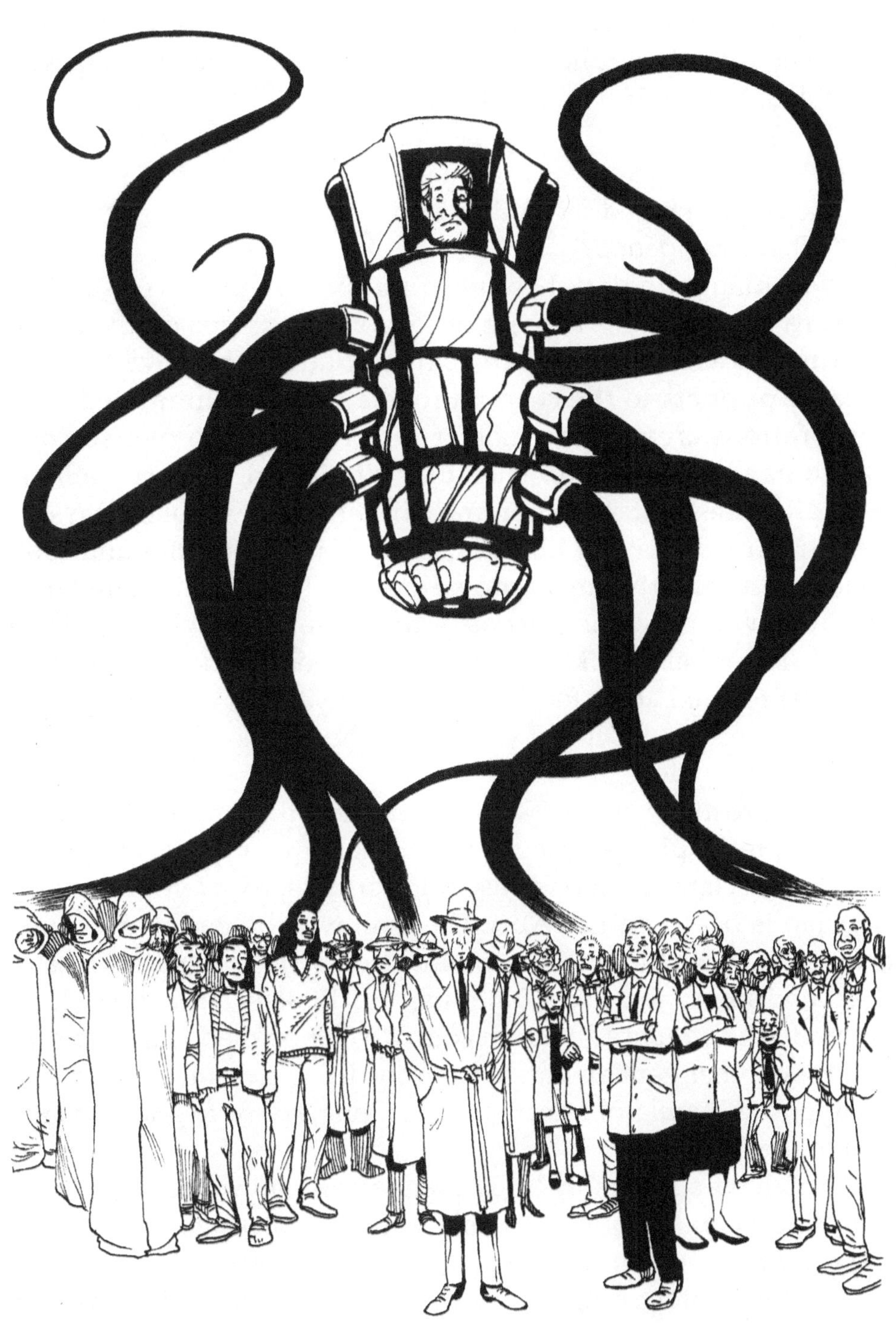

"Eighty-five years after the rise of conformity," the tiny woman said. The man they called the Great One tried to take a step and stumbled, but the Hagee caught him.

"It's an honor, sir. Welcome back. We've never needed you more."

The Hagee helped the author into a chair.

"What's happened?"

A woman with dark hair, wearing full-length gloves stepped forward and bowed. "The rise of corporations signaled the fall of freedom in what was once the United States. The governments became puppets to the corporations and were eliminated. The corporations created the master programmers to oversee our day-to-day infrastructure. Then they eliminated the corporations. Soon after, the master programmers began to slowly take away our personal freedoms and liberties. They burned libraries and took control of all entertainment programming. They manipulated it so that it served only one purpose—to praise those who ruled the world. The rebels hid key people in cryopods in hopes that they could be revived at a later date to fight the masters. We have been searching for you for many years, sir," the Wan said.

"Me? Why me?"

"Because many of your writings survived the burnings and they continue to inspire people. In truth, there are a great number of Henderson clans, each one based on some aspect of your writing. My clan is based on Lai Wan. The man who helped you to your chair is a Hagee, those who were inspired by Jack Hagee. We have the Londoners, the Piers Knights, the Blakely and Boles. The woman who prepared your cryopod to be opened is a Wezleski and these other gentlemen are from the Ministry of Extraordinary Weapons. We will not be safe here for long, so we're going to take you to the *Roosevelt*."

"You have a spaceship?" C.J. Henderson said with a huge smile and almost childlike glee. His Rocky and Noodles tales were set on a spaceship of the same name.

"Unfortunately not, but we did acquire an aircraft carrier. It serves as a mobile base. We renamed it after the ship in your Rocky and Noodles stories. The clan we use to try and mislead the media follows the works of Marv Richards and is doing their best to block the master programmers from finding us, but we don't have long. As soon as you're able, we have to move. The Conformity Police may send in another team after the first. We need to be gone before they get here and for all we know, reinforcements may already be on the way," the Hagee said.

C.J. Henderson stood, unsteady at first, but he took one wobbly step, then another.

"Sir, are you sure you're okay?" the Wan said.

"I'm no stranger to pain. Let's go."

"Sir, I realize you've only just woken but we've been awaiting your return for years. Each of the clans believes that you're the key to inspiring the people to rise up and take back our world. Please, it would mean so much to us if you could tell us what your plan is. Do we need to start gathering weapons or people? What do you want us to do?"

"You have a way to distribute information?"

"The master programmers completely control the electronic and digital media, but we still have a number of printing facilities," the man with the goggles said. "We at the Ministry saved them from the master programmers' reign of destruction."

"Excellent. Then I know what to do. Get me to a keyboard."

C.J. had a knack for sweeping those around him up in his enthusiasm. One moment you were having an innocent conversation about movies or the fate of society, the next you are happily agreeing to write a story or edit a collection. Oft times, if you rose to that challenge something wonderful resulted, something you did not think you had in you.

The Editors

C.J. didn't plan to inspire or motivate. He figured a writer had to want it enough to motivate themselves. But what he did like to do is push and egg people on, force them past those comfortable boundaries. What C.J. liked to do was throw down gauntlets then wait to see what happened next. *In the Dying Light* is a gauntlet story. One year when we were carpooling to Balticon C.J. and I were chatting away and somehow we got onto the topic of cross-genre. Don't ask me how the conversation went, I couldn't tell you, but what I can tell you is that it ended with me being challenged to write a Lovecraftian romance in space. Read *In the Dying Light*, then judge for yourself if I rose to the challenge sufficiently.

Danielle Ackley-McPhail

In the Dying Light

An Alliance Archives Adventure

Danielle Ackley-McPhail

EARTH ORBIT: 42.05.18 – 0715HRS
On the command deck of the Stellar Clipper *McKay*, First Officer Ushimi Yakata ran the final checklist before third shift ended:

DUTY LOG: 42.05.18 – 0715HRS, YAKATA, U.
REACTOR STATUS – NOMINAL;
O_2 LEVELS – OPTIMAL;
POWER – FIVE PERCENT OVER-CONSUMPTION.

She frowned at the last item as she printed out a hard copy of the entry. *We're going to have to watch our calculations,* she thought. *We haven't even left orbit and already the systems are running hot.*

It was that damn shuttle Corporate had them balancing on the *McKay*'s nose. They were hauling the spacer's equivalent of a luxury yacht over twelve light years to Demeter just so some CEO could tour his colonial facilities in style...There were much more important payloads they could have taken with them. Of course, it was the "pay" part that decided things in the end; the rates for transporting luxury items to the Tau Ceti system were ten times that of necessary goods.

Behind her a *clunk* and a soft *whoosh* announced the arrival of her replacement. A whiff of licorice drifted from close by her ear. She'd stopped counting the times she had told Karl Dunn not to crowd her. A prime example of why they had a history and no future. She'd had doubts about signing him for this cruise. They had been close once, very close. But not anymore. And with only a nine-man crew, she had no hope of avoiding him.

Her lips pressed in a tight, thin line, Yakata dropped her hand to the toggle by her hip and shifted the command chair back along its track, away from the control panel.

"Hey! Watch it!"

She brought the chair around, her grey eyes leveled dead on at Karl as he rubbed his abdomen where the chair smacked into him. Only his grip on the nearby tether bar kept him bobbing in place.

"Excuse me," she said, her tone cool and formal. "I didn't realize you were so close."

The flat, persistent tone of the proximity warning sounded through the cabin, interrupting any comment Karl would have made. They both forgot their personal conflict, their attention riveted on the sensors.

Toggling the command chair back into place, Yakata automatically scanned the ship's attitude and power consumption on the screens flanking the main monitor. At the same time, she called up the isometric collision display. The flashing alert icon vanished from the screen in front of her. In its place appeared a wire-frame sphere with a representation of the *McKay* in the center. Something closed on the ship from behind, moving at a fraction of a meter per second. They had about thirty minutes until it came into range over their drive section.

"Dunn, reach over and activate the aft camera," Yakata ordered as her fingers danced in and out of the button depressions on the control panel. At her command, the main display switched from short-range to long-range scanning. She had to be sure whatever approached was not the forward edge of a meteor storm or something else their ablative hull plating could not handle.

Her scans told her nothing more. She called to Karl, "Crewman, do we have visual?"

Silence.

"Crewman..." Her short, sharp tone telegraphed impatience. "Do...we... have...visual?"

She whipped around, spearing him with a glare. He remained oblivious, his feet tucked into the boot docks and his gaze riveted on the image on the external monitoring station.

What the hell? Yakata had never seen him like this. He looked stunned...horrified. What could be out there?

Remembering the fate of her father's freighter, the *Tyler*, she felt a shiver of dread. Not another wreck...

She couldn't tell; Karl's body blocked the screen. Impatiently, she released the restraint keeping her in the command chair and drifted out. Once she cleared the panel, she rotated and pulled herself toward Karl.

"Step aside, crewman," she barked.

His intent gaze snapped to her. Emotions rippled violently across his face, darkening his deep brown eyes to nearly black. It unsettled her, but Yakata didn't back off. Dunn's moods were nothing new to her. He had always been too on edge, his emotions close to the surface; like he picked up on random vibes in the air that no one else could feel. In their time together, she had never been able to tell what a given situation would trigger. Now she told herself she didn't really care. She kept her expression impassive and her gaze sharp. "Move it...now."

The muscles along Karl's jaw twitched and his eyes fell out of focus. He closed them and gave his head a little shake. She could see the tension drain away. When he opened his eyes again, they reflected faint confusion. Without a word, he gave the standard heel jerk to free his feet from the workstation's dock and drifted off to the side.

She gave him a measured look before redirecting her attention to the screen. The camera completed deployment, the high-power, one-hundred-optical zoom fully engaged. What a stunning view. Distant stars glittered like metallic flecks on a field of raw black silk and muted colors added an unexpected depth to the starscape. Pretty sights didn't interest her, though. She scanned for her objective with an intensity that mirrored Karl's earlier stance.

The projectile headed toward them wasn't some random bit of space debris; it was clearly manufactured. The shape appeared something like a squat pillar or obelisk, and appeared to be about the size of her head. It was too far away to make out much more, though the camera hinted at intricate detail.

Rogue thoughts of her father swarmed her mind once more. In his last letter to her, he mentioned a similar find. She'd lost him long before the letter ever reached her. Neither her father, nor the object had been retrieved. Burned into her memory, as clear as yesterday, was the image of his shattered helmet found floating in the vacuum of space. She still had that helmet.

She banished the thought. Turning back to Karl, Yakata caught his eye and held it. "Assume your post. I'm heading up to the rendezvous station to retrieve the object."

He remained silent a moment. His jaw ticked and his gaze flickered from the aft display to her face.

" 'Ta..." he began, but she cut him off.

"Excuse me, crewman, how did you address me?"

"Ma'am," he ground out through clenched teeth, frustration snapping in his eyes. "Respectfully, I'm not sure that you should... something feels really wrong about this."

"I have to do this."

The knowing look he gave her disconcerted Yakata. If anyone understood, he did. She didn't like that familiarity or the self-betraying warmth she felt at his concern. "I said get to your post. Start the pre-hyperdrive checklist," she ordered. "The captain wants to jump by 0800."

She pulled her communications hood up over her close-cropped ebony hair and triggered the overhead hatch. With the grace of frequent practice, she hauled herself up through the shaft. Propelling herself past the T-junction that branched off toward the cargo bay, she opened the second hatch into the rendezvous station. She closed it behind her before drifting toward the aft window. Yakata pressed the activation button on the left side of her comm hood. "Command deck..."

A sharp chirp sounded before Karl responded, his voice slightly staticy. "Go ahead, ma'am."

"I need an update on the incoming object."

There was a pause. While she waited, Yakata peered out into space, as if she had any chance of pinpointing the object without the aid of the cameras. It drew closer, but not that close.

Another chirp brought her out of her distraction.

"Ma'am?"

"Go ahead, crewman."

"The object is ten minutes out and closing."

"Acknowledged," she responded, and cut the connection.

Ten minutes. Barely enough time to deploy the arm. She snapped her boots into the docks and engaged the control panel. Powering up the arm, she then hit the sequence instructing it to retrieve the grappling attachment. While the mechanism prepared, she triggered the cargo bay doors. A strident warning klaxon sounded as a large segment of the ship opened to space. The arm rose from its cradle in slow, precise movements. Her teeth gritted and her muscles tensed as she watched. It had to move faster or she would miss the interception point. With her free hand, she depressed the activator on her comm hood once more.

"Command deck..."

"Go ahead, ma'am."

"Feed me the trajectory of the object."

On the panel in front of her, a micro-display came to life. The information played across it. This was going to be close. She deployed the grappling net to intersect the flight path and held her breath. The object crested the drive section in a gentle arc, and seemed to flare as it came into contact with the sun's rays, bathing the ship and arm in a startling green glow. It faded in the shadow of the arm. Yakata leaned into the console. It appeared her prize might overshoot the net. Reaching for the joystick in front of her, she extended the assembly as high as it would go over the drive section.

Her breath hitched. It still looked at risk of skimming past. *This is ridiculous. It's space debris. There's no reason I should be so upset.*

She tried shifting the joystick even further, but the arm had reached full extension.

Her father's face drifted unbidden across her thoughts. It felt like she had failed him...again. She clenched her teeth and forced the thought away. Furious blinking cleared her vision, but she could hardly believe what she saw: the object changed trajectory. The alteration was slight; barely perceptible except for the drive section acting as a point of reference. Still, Yakata had to wonder if she had really seen it. This was impossible. The thing could not have changed its trajectory. Short of mechanical means or an outside intervention, an object moving in space would continue along the same path until it encountered another force. And yet, as the artifact plowed into the grappling net, she forgot all about the laws of physics. The net closed, locking the object into place.

"Yeah!" she cried out, the sound loud and unbridled in the seclusion of the rendezvous station. Only the boot docks kept her from bouncing around the compartment. "Oh, yeah!"

A burst of unexpected static crackled from her comm hood. She felt the blood drain from her face as she went still.

"Hey! Knock it off!" Karl's amused voice came over the connection she'd forgotten to close. "You want to rupture my ear drum?"

"My apologies, crewman," she responded with a degree of dignity she did not currently feel. "The object has been retrieved. I'm locking down and securing the salvage."

She cut the connection.

Shoving embarrassment aside, Yakata input the sequence that returned the arm to its cradle. Another rapid set of keystrokes, and the cargo bay doors closed. She grew impatient with the drawn-out procedure. Recklessness in vacuum, however, could get a spacer killed.

Once everything was locked down, she retreated to the antechamber to climb into her protective constrictor suit. She waited for the green light from the automatic systems check before securing her helmet and engaging the O_2 tanks. Prepped for EVA, Yakata cycled through the airlock into the cargo bay.

She grabbed an empty storage container and hauled both it and herself down the length of the armature. Once there, she anchored the container to the deck and pulled herself up the handholds along the wall until she drew even with the grappling attachment. She hit the release and worked the fingers open.

Her hands twitched over the surface of the artifact and she had to resist the urge to draw off her suit's skin-tight gloves. The object demanded to be caressed.

In shape it resembled a short, squat obelisk. It tapered slightly from top to bottom and had three columns of unfamiliar symbols running up and down each side. It was metal...apparently old metal, given the deep, dull sheen. The color had a greenish tinge, like ancient bronze. Only this was no metal she recognized. It seemed smooth, almost soft, other than the etching. Otherwise, there were no seams or depressions.

It took extreme effort to lower the thing into the bin. Now was not the time to examine it. She had less than ten minutes to get herself secured for hyperdrive. Unhitching the container, she hefted it to her shoulder and propelled herself toward the airlock. In the antechamber, she slid her burden into a storage locker by the cargo bay hatch and keyed it to her personal code. It would be safe until she could take it down to the lab.

DUTY LOG: 42.05.18 – 1100HRS, MABERRY, CAPTAIN J.

REACTOR STATUS – NOMINAL;

O_2 LEVELS – 98 PERCENT;

POWER – TEN PERCENT OVER-CONSUMPTION

NOTE: SCHEDULE DIAGNOSTICS OF SHIP'S SYSTEMS UPON ARRIVAL AT DEMETER, *McKAY* EXHIBITING SYSTEMS-WIDE REDUCTION IN EFFICIENCY DESPITE RECENT OVERHAUL. POWER FLUCTUATIONS SHIP-WIDE, STABILIZED. MALFUNCTION OF ATMOSPHERIC FILTERS IN COMPARTMENTS 8A THROUGH C, CORRECTED. ELECTRICAL FIRES BETWEEN BULKHEADS 10 AND 11, SECTION 5, CONTAINED; DAMAGE MINIMAL.

CARGO BAY ANTECHAMBER: 42.05.18 – 1100HRS

Yakata struggled for hours to get some rest. She just couldn't do it, though. The artifact haunted her thoughts. She would almost say it called to her, but that was as nuts as thinking it had changed its trajectory. She tossed and fussed until Jackson and Pittman, the crewmembers trying to sleep in the billets flanking hers, begged her to give up.

That was why she climbed back down into the cargo bay antechamber again. Captain Maberry, in position on the command deck, had given her a considering look, but didn't question her. She'd already briefed him about the events that occurred at the end of her shift.

All thought of anything but the artifact fled her mind as she pushed open the last hatch and continued down the ladder, which in orbit had been the floor. She hated the way hyperdrive and the artificial gravity it created turned reality perpendicular to orbital conditions. Kneeling down, she punched her code with rapid jabs and hauled open the storage locker at her feet.

Any thought of spatial geometry evaporated.

Yakata half expected the artifact to be a dream. But there it was, nestled in its bin. She tried to draw it out of the locker.

It wouldn't budge. In the weightlessness of the orbiting ship, the artifact had been nothing to move. Now that they were under drive there was artificial gravity again. Not earth-norm, but enough that they could walk on the deck. If the obelisk was this heavy in three-quarters grav, she didn't want to consider what it would be like under normal conditions. It had to be denser than gold.

No! Yakata straddled the opening, flexed her knees, and inch by inch pulled the container up, until sweat ran into her eyes and her muscles screamed. She was not waiting forty-eight hours until they were in orbit.

PERSONAL LOG ENTRY: 42.05.18 – 1230HRS, DUNN, K.

WE RETRIEVED SOMETHING TODAY. 'TA...EXCUSE ME...FIRST OFFICER USHIMI HASN'T TOLD ME WHAT IT IS. DON'T THINK SHE EVEN KNOWS. WHILE I WAS ON SHIFT, SHE TOOK IT TO THE STOR-

AGE BAY CAPTAIN HAD TEMPORARILY CONVERTED INTO A LAB. SHE TALKED O'NEAL, THE METALLURGIST WE'RE SHEPARDING TO DEMETER, INTO HELPING HER TRY TO FIGURE OUT WHAT IT IS.

SHE GOES ON SHIFT IN SEVEN HOURS, BUT THEY'RE STILL HOLED UP IN THAT LAB. SHE'S GOING TO BE A REAL BITCH ON DECK TONIGHT IF SHE DOESN'T GET SOME SLEEP, BUT SHE'S OBSESSING ON THAT BIT OF DEBRIS.

OF COURSE, I CAN'T STOP THINKING ABOUT IT EITHER. IT'S GOTTEN UNDER MY SKIN. IT SHOULDN'T BE ON THIS SHIP! IT HAS ME SO FREAKED, AND I CAN'T EVEN TELL WHY. THE FIRST HALF-HOUR OF MY SHIFT IS A LOST MEMORY. ALL I KNOW IS THAT IT FEELS LIKE WE ARE IN FOR A MAJOR SHITSTORM.

TEMPORARY SCIENCE LAB: 42.05.18 – 1230HRS

"What in the world made Corporate think it was worth the 100-million-dollar ticket to haul you up here?" Yakata growled through clenched teeth. Even as she said it, her hindbrain winced.

Bastian O'Neal, world-renowned metallurgist, lowered his instruments to the work surface and gave her a long, silent look. The dignified expression on his ebony face didn't change, but his hazel eyes were disapproving. He didn't answer. He looked away and took up the artifact in both latex-covered hands, repositioning it for another documenting photograph.

She'd strained to haul her prize down here; he seemed to toss it about as if it were cotton candy. Part of that was due to his clearly prosthetic left arm; but part had to be because of his own innate strength. Someone who didn't know better could be excused for thinking he mined metals, rather than studying them.

The metallurgist set aside his digital camera and picked up the item once more. He turned it in his hands until he'd looked at every side, his finger lingered over the engraving. She wanted to snatch it from his grasp. Uncontrollably, a muscle in her forehead twitched, as did her fingers. How dare he manhandle her salvage like that, hefting it with an ease that she couldn't? She tensed and fought not to scowl at him. What was wrong with her?

Yakata tried to shake it off. This was O'Neal's field. She'd come to him for help and he was kind enough to give it. She should be grateful and respectful, at the very least. It wasn't like her to behave this way. She took a deep breath and forced herself to calm, to offer an apologetic smile and be pleasant.

Finally, O'Neal set the artifact down. Yakata expected to relax. Instead, she tensed even more; ready, in fact, to hurry forward and grab the obelisk away. But then O'Neal spoke, distracting her.

"I can't identify it."

"What do you mean you can't identify it?!"

"The tests were unable to determine the age or composition of the material."

Her resolve to be polite evaporated. "What did Corporate do... send you up here as a tax write-off?"

Seething with frustration, Yakata grabbed for her artifact.

O'Neal stepped in her way.

"If you're done insulting me?

"There's one more test I can run, but I need some equipment from the storage bay. My imaging spectrometer is our last option on-ship."

She glared at him and had to force her negativity down. It was harder to do. Without a word, Yakata moved to the terminal set into the chamber wall, her feet straddling the boot docks.

The muscles in her shoulders bunched and tightened as she keyed in the commands calling up the ship's manifest. He watched her. Surely plotting to take her salvage for himself.

Whoa! Where did that paranoia come from? She forced it away.

Finally, she located his equipment and requested immediate retrieval. Closing out the screen, she whirled to face him. For a moment, everything held a greenish tinge like the one she'd noted when the object crested the drive section. The sense of looming increased with the glow. It faded so quickly, though, that she had to wonder if it were her vision causing the effect. That would explain the flickers out of the corner of her eye. Yakata clenched her eyes shut and popped her neck. It sounded like several rounds of gunfire.

"Sorry, O'Neal, can't imagine why I'm so edgy. Jackson will bring your spectrometer down in short order. Why don't you head to the mess for some coffee...I'll comm you when the equipment gets here."

"That's okay. If I'm here when it arrives I can hook it into the ship's systems quicker. This has already taken longer..."

"O'Neal," Yakata cut him off, her tone sharp and brittle, even to her own ears. "Go get some coffee. I'll have the spectrometer rigged up when you get here."

For a moment, she thought he would refuse. Her suspicions flared brighter and she had to consciously force her fists not to clench. She didn't trust him here; didn't want him here, unless he was in the middle of a test. Even then she had issues.

Her gaze again locked with his. She read concern in his eyes. But did something else lurk beneath that? Something sly? Calculating? Damnit! She couldn't tell! It took more effort to mimic something of a reasonable tone. "I have to be here to sign off on the retrieval. If you don't want any coffee, could you at least get me some? I'm dying here."

TEMPORARY SCIENCE LAB: 42.05.18 – 1245HRS

Yakata vibrated with impatience as O'Neal finished calibrating the spectrometer. She wanted to snatch his hands away from the knobs and buttons and yell at him to get on with it. It wasn't just an overwhelming need to know. That she could have handled. No, it was more like whatever lurked behind her drew closer, just out of sight, just out of hearing range. Always there, always watching... Some part of her equated it with the artifact. She had to know what it was now, but the technology would do them no good if it weren't set up properly. She understood that.

Then why was she ready to scream when he slipped a common bit of steel in the spherical sample chamber and fired up the machine?

She couldn't restrain herself any more. "Come on, already!"

"Do you want accurate results, or do you just want me to go through the motions?" O'Neal's voice came out a low, controlled rumble, contrasting sharply with her outburst. "If you don't care if the results are accurate, you're wasting my time and I'm out of here."

His response made Yakata want to scream even more, but he was right. What was wrong with her? Her impatience did not serve either one of them well and she couldn't afford to have him abandon the test. She could probably figure out the machine, but the data it spit out would be indecipherable to her.

Taking a deep breath, she forced herself to calm.

"Sorry."

It took a lot of effort not to fidget as O'Neal watched her closely a moment. The concern had returned, along with a thread of irritation. He clearly wanted this to be done as much as she did, even if their reasons were different. Without a word, he turned back to the spectrometer.

"Okay, we're ready."

Yakata's pulse sped up. She reached for the artifact, only to flinch back as a mild static arced between it and her fingertips. It seemed to cling to her hand like the persistent suction of vacuum through a hull breach. Like something tried to suck her out the tiniest hole, only the hard surface of reality kept her from going through. Before she could say something, the pull abruptly released and a surge of rage and frustration swelled over her. She shook it off. Looked up in a daze. O'Neal had lifted her prize away and slid it into the chamber in place of the metal bar. He made no comment and Yakata saw no sparks when he touched it. Had the phenomenon been her imagination? She couldn't resist creeping forward to glance at the operator's display as the spectrometer charged up to pulse full-spectrum light at the object from six points within the sphere.

The hum of the machine seemed to come up through the deck plates until she expected her entire body to vibrate with it. A flaring light intensified abruptly until it engulfed the machine and the room. The power surged and the deck plates vibrated more violently beneath Yakata's feet. Both she and O'Neal flinched in that instance of brilliance before they were engulfed by utter darkness. The only sound was a sharp gasp. She couldn't tell which of them it came from. She could no longer hear the spectrometer or any of the ship's normal background mechanical noises. Other than their nervous breathing, silence dominated the pitch black.

Yakata struggled not to panic. Where was the hum of the hyperdrive? The click of relays opening and closing? The sizzling snap of the comms? Sounds every spacer took for granted; their unrealized security blanket in everlasting night.

Yakata shuddered.

The darkness seemed to last forever; in truth it was less than twenty seconds before systems re-engaged with a whir. Not even long enough for them to fall out of drive.

Right on the heels of everything powering up, all comms within hearing distance gave a strident chirp.

"...eport...All crew, report!"

She reached for the comm on the console and toggled the activator to respond to Captain Maberry.

"Yakata here. O'Neal and I are in the Science Lab."

"What the hell was that?"

Yakata didn't have an answer. She couldn't have gotten one in, anyway, as a stream of responses came over the comm. All crew were accounted for.

"Everyone to stations, run full diagnostics. Let's figure out what the deal is before it happens again," Captain Maberry ordered before closing the comm line.

Turning to O'Neal, Yakata noted the confusion on his face as he looked at the read-out from the spectrometer.

"What? Something go wrong?"

O'Neal turned toward her, his head shaking. "The test completed before everything shut down, but this doesn't make sense."

She walked over and read the printout:

PROCESSING ERROR 021:
SPECTRAL ANOMALY – NEGATIVE SCAN

"*Kuso shite shinezo!*" Yakata hissed through clenched teeth.

O'Neal looked at her oddly. "I don't know what you just said, but it sounded painful."

Yakata flushed. Among spacers cursing was one thing, profanity was a part of their make-up. But in front of others she generally conducted herself more circumspectly. She was just grateful the man did not speak Japanese.

"I apologize for my rudeness. But, damn!" She slammed her hand down on the casing of the machine. "All of that and it's unidentifiable!"

"Not just unidentifiable...it's like nothing's there. The machine didn't even register the walls of the chamber." His expression grew considering. "It's as if the artifact absorbed the light. But to do so this completely...it's impossible for none to have gotten past it."

"Malfunction?"

"Not one I've ever seen, but there's one way to find out."

Captain Maberry had ordered everyone to their stations. But she had to know. She could always double-time it to the command deck.

O'Neal opened the chamber and reached for the artifact. He hissed sharply, as if in pain. His body arched and shuddered. The look of terror in his eyes sent panic through Yakata. It must be the prosthetic. She remembered the static that had clung to her hand when she'd touched the artifact earlier.

Yakata yanked an equipment bag toward her and rapidly rifled through it. Tucked in the bottom she found a set of insulated gauntlets. She donned them and braced herself against the workstation. With all her weight behind the effort, she hauled on the obelisk until it left his grasp. It came away with the sound of metal scraping metal. Yakata landed in a heap across the compartment, the obelisk heavy on her chest. O'Neal collapsed across the table, greenish static arcing and popping along the length of his arm. He shook his head and groaned. After a moment, he leveled a glare toward Yakata.

Perhaps it was the sparks, or perhaps just the light, but as he stared at her in silence, it seemed his eyes reflected the green hue.

He slowly stood and stalked across the room to where she lay. When he reached out his hand, her eyes went wide, expecting pain.

She searched his face for some clue as the man remained silent. His eyes darkened and she couldn't read the swirl of emotions dancing through them. She shivered. He closed his eyes with a sigh. When he opened them all she saw was impatience in their green depth. Green? But....

"The gauntlets..."

She yanked them off and held them up, never taking her eyes from him. He donned the gear and lifted the artifact from her chest. She gasped as breath flooded back into her lungs to full capacity. Damn, that thing was heavy, she swore to herself.

O'Neal turned his back to her. He deposited the obelisk on a metal tray on the table and reinserted the control element he'd used to test the machine initially.

The second reading of the steel bar was identical to the first.

Without a word, Yakata returned the artifact to its storage locker. Using her body as a shield, she keyed the lock with her personal code.

She turned and found O'Neal staring at her. Yakata carefully slipped past him and hurried from the compartment, trying to ignore the faint odor of scorched latex lingering in her nostrils.

Personal Log Entry: 42.05.18 – 1250hrs, Dunn, K.

McKay's systems just flatlined. Everything's back up, but talk about freaking out. What the hell is going on?

Haven't felt like this since I was four and Da took me to the reptile house at the Bronx Zoo. I zoomed all over that place. Couldn't stay still...until I came to the king cobra. Something had pissed it off. It mantled and swayed three feet high in the air, right up close to the glass. It kept up a hiss, low and menacing. Don't know how long I stood there watching its tongue flicker in and out above me, but I couldn't move. Not even when it struck. Lightning-fast it slammed into the glass. To this day, I swear its fangs left long grooves in the surface, dripping with venom.

I still remember the stench of terror. Right now it's strong in my nose…a hundred times stronger than it was when I was four. And I have that feeling again…like death is hovering above my head and I'm not sure if the glass is going to hold.

Damn…Captain just called duty stations.

Command Deck: 42.05.18 – 1310hrs

Yakata hauled herself through the command deck hatch from the *McKay's* main shaft into a tangible silence. The shaft ran the length of the ship and was fitted out with a ladder that doubled as a track for the slow-moving utility lift. The track could either be climbed or used for crewmen to pull themselves along, depending on the ship's attitude. She had scaled it at record speed, but apparently she hadn't been quick enough.

"First Officer Ushimi…the comm system may have been affected by the anomaly. My order to report to duty stations doesn't seem to have reached all compartments." The captain's words were even and void of tension. His gaze was not. The look he gave her was harder than the artifact she'd left in the lab. "With this sudden glitch, I'm concerned that diagnostics might not show up all malfunctions. I'll need you to conduct an on-site inspection of every comm station and hood on the *McKay*."

Yakata flinched on the inside. "Yes, sir. Right away, sir."

Captain Maberry was known for his swift and fitting discipline. Actually, she'd gotten off easy; she should have been the first on the deck, not counting those who were already there.

There was a sound beneath her feet. She stepped aside to clear the hatch. An acrid aroma preceded Dunn as he clambered to his post.

"Ah, very good." The captain's smile was not very pleasant, though his tone seemed to be. "Crewman Dunn will assist you."

Drive Section Service Module: 42.05.18 – 1700hrs

This was it. The final comm station on her half of the list. Yakata sighed as she pulled out the checklist and ran the last test. Carefully, she removed the housing then used her Fenix utility light and a telescoping mirror to visually inspect the wiring. After that she tested the connections. Finally, she closed the unit and toggled the activator.

"Dunn..."

"Go ahead..."

"Drive section comm inspection complete, how are you coming with the Engineering unit?"

"System's green to go." Dunn's voice remained even but Yakata detected an edge to it. It was barely perceptible, but his breath came out in quick, shallow huffs. She waited for him to report something catastrophic, but he remained silent.

"Okay, that's all of them. Wait for me at the main shaft." Yakata cut the link and toggled the activator again. "Command deck..."

"Go ahead." The captain's voice came through the relay sharp and precise. Yakata winced. He would remain on deck until she relieved him. That was part of what drove home the lesson. Her failure to follow orders affected everyone, right up to the captain, whom she respected more than anyone alive. Nothing, short of a fatality, would have made her feel worse about her lapse in protocol.

"On-site inspection of the communications system complete," Yakata responded, keeping her voice neutral.

"Acknowledged. I'll be waiting to hear your report."

"Yes, sir." Yakata groaned as she cut the link.

With haste, she secured her maintenance kit on her hip, slid the flashlight into its belt loop, and left the compartment. The sensors flanking the door registered her exit. The drive room went dark and the dim, stand-by lights of the causeway brightened. After nearly a decade of service, she generally took the lighting system for granted. Today she newly appreciated the comfort it represented. Even without the recent system's failure, Yakata was uneasy. Her nerves vibrated beneath the surface of her skin and her eyes ached from trying to penetrate the dark spaces around her. She'd yet to spy anything staring back. Her skin crawled though as she imagined a thousand pairs of eyes creeping forward into the now-darkened room behind her. Clenching her teeth, she cocked her head from side to side until the vertebrae ceased to pop. To her left, she thought she heard the faintest sound from somewhere near the pressurized tanks. Probably a loose valve. She made note of the section where she suspected the leak, and set off for the main shaft.

Dunn was not at the rendezvous.

Toggling the activator on her comm hood, the barest edge of anger sharpened her tone. "Crewman Dunn, report..."

Silence.

"Dunn, what is your location?"

Still no response.

What in the world was going on? Their personal comm hoods were the first to be tested. Both had operated fine. She went to the comm screen in the main shaft wall. With a couple of jabs she input the protocol that instructed the system to display the current location of all crewmembers.

She glanced down the list of names and locations: Captain Maberry and Crewman Suarez—Command deck; Crewmen Jackson and Chapman—Environmental Control Compartment; Specialist O'Neal —Temporary Science Lab; Crewmen Pittman, Jenks, and Gunter—Mess hall; and Crewman Dunn...

Port lateral airlock! Yakata powered down the display and set off back the way she came at a hard clip.

Bad enough they'd both drawn discipline duty, reporting back late would be impossible for the captain to gloss over this time. She tried her comm hood again, activating it with such force she could feel the surrounding fabric pull. "Crewman Dunn...respond..."

Nothing. She put on a little more speed through the shaft. A tight sensation took root in her gut. She tried again, "Come on, Dunn, talk to me. What's going on?"

No answer. The airlocks came into sight. Even in the dim light of the corridor, she could see a dark smear on the floor.

"Dunn! Damnit, Karl! Answer me!"

Yakata closed the last few meters. Dropping to one knee, she touched a finger to the slick spot. It came away bright red, the sweet, metallic tang unmistakable.

What happened? And where was Dunn? Sensors indicated the port airlock, but both chambers were dark. There should be lights. Lighting was automatic. She stepped to the side of the hatch portal and reached for her flashlight. The high-powered beam cut through the black pit beyond the glass.

Yakata gasped. For a second she could do nothing but stand there and stare at the horror revealed by the light: an EVA suit sprawled against the far wall, blood a solid curtain across the faceplate of the helmet.

A burst of static reminded her that the comm hood was still active, on stand-by. The sound snapped her out of the shock.

"Command deck..." She was surprised how low and calm her voice remained. The rest of her trembled. "Command deck, acknowledge...."

The only response was another burst of static.

She moved to the comm unit in the corridor wall and tried again. Again static hissed and crackled through the corridor, echoing through her comm hood. She moved back to the airlock door.

The beam of light glimmered on the helmet like sunlight through rubies. She could make out nothing beyond the faceplate. Swallowing hard, she swept the airlock with light as far as she could from side to side. Nothing. Not even more smears. No movement. Still, something did this. Yakata was acutely aware of the blind spots to either side of the hatch.

She punched in the sequence to open the airlock. The keypad didn't respond. She tightened her grip on the flashlight. It was awkward manipulating the manual release one-handed, but, with determination, she managed it. The hatch opened smoothly. Out wafted the heavy, copper-penny scent of blood and something else, something bitter and sharp. The lights still didn't engage.

"Dunn, can you respond?"

She peered into the room, her head just past the collar as she flashed the light into the corner to the right of the door. Nothing.

As she brought her light around to the other side, the comm hood gave a more energetic hiss. She flinched back at the unexpected sound. A blur of motion from the left caught her eye. Metal slammed against metal. From the shadows, hoarse breathing punched up into a roar. She now recognized the acrid odor in the air. She'd smelt it on the command deck, when Dunn came up the hatch.

There wasn't time to call out to him. There was only time to move. An industrial-grade spanner crashed into the airlock door just millimeters away from her head. Again, the weapon rose. She couldn't continue to evade; not in this restricted space. She brought the utility light up to block the spanner's descent and allowed her body to fall back upon the deck. The move cost her the light, which went spinning away, but her bones were intact.

She stared up into Dunn's face. He was barely recognizable. His eyes were wide and wild, a long, bloody scratch marred his face, and sweat stood out in hard beads on his forehead. The rest of him was coated in blood. He did not seem to recognize her. She watched as a tremor ran through his body. No matter what had passed between them, she didn't want to hurt him, not even to get away. She would, but she didn't want to. She prayed he came out of it.

"Dunn…Karl, what happened to you?"

She held her breath. For a moment his pupils expanded. Recognition floated just beneath the surface. Then her comm hood hissed. His echoed in response. She had most of a second to watch him retreat behind the terror.

"Oh shit!" Yakata braced herself. This was going to hurt. Her only hope lay in the leverage of her position and her greater lower-body strength. The spanner came down full force. She dodged her torso as best she could, but took a glancing blow to her shoulder. Her left side went numb on impact. She wrapped herself around the spanner with her good arm and drew her legs up sharp. Snarling, she planted both feet in Dunn's gut and shoved for all she was worth.

The weapon remained in her possession, though it was close. Dunn went flying. Yakata winced as he crashed into the lockers, landing awkwardly on the sprawled EVA suit. She bit her lip at the fresh smear of blood across the dented metal. Bit harder against the impulse to go to him. Instead, she rolled to her feet and slammed the airlock hatch. Using the spanner, she wedged the door closed as best she could. It wouldn't hold long. She headed for the main shaft at a hard clip. Within the first five strides, the pain in her left arm triggered a grey haze across her vision. Gasping, she stopped running immediately.

Yakata blinked furiously, forcing herself to take slow, deep breaths, until the haze went away. Behind her she could hear banging, enraged and violent.

Gritting her teeth against the pain, she loosened her web belt and slipped the wrist of her damaged arm into the gap between belt and pants, angled across her stomach. She hissed with the pain and the sounds from the airlock increased in intensity.

She forced Dunn out of her thoughts and tightened the belt against her wrist, immobilizing the damaged arm as best she could. Once again, she set off, this time at a gentler, swinging lope. Her gut clenched. As she left the cacophony of the drive section behind, the faint sound of a warning klaxon could be heard elsewhere on the ship.

Yakata toggled her comm activator again. "Command deck... Come in, Captain Maberry." Not even a hiss sounded in her ear. "Deck officer, respond."

No answer; and her comm went dead, completely dead.

Abandoning her gentle pace, Yakata ran full out for the transport. The lift was slow, but one-handed, she would be even slower hauling herself up the ladder to the command deck. Her eyes locked on the lift mooring as it came into sight. The knots in her shoulders eased the slightest increment. The platform was there. She added another burst of speed.

Her steps faltered as she drew close. Something was not right. The lift wasn't seated properly in the track. It hovered about six inches off the mooring. She stopped where she was and tried to peer beneath it.

How had she missed the thin, crimson rivulets snaking across the deck? The fine, meandering tributaries flowing from the crushed body of Crewman Dave Jackson? Yakata fought the urge to be sick.

Was Dunn responsible? Was this why he wasn't at the rendezvous? Why he didn't answer her hails? Her throat spasmed and she had to swallow hard as she moved closer to examine the mechanism.

The body was tangled in the power couplings, bits of it pulped by the gears. Even if she could get the lift into motion, it would shred what was left of him. Only his face was untouched. His expression would haunt her.

A sound echoed up the corridor. Cursing, Yakata re-tightened her belt against her injured arm and climbed onto the lift. Her added force caused the platform to drop another inch. There was a sickening crack as something organic gave. She clenched her teeth and closed her eyes, emptied her mind of everything, and started up the lift. Before it had gone more than a few meters she slumped to her knees.

Central Shaft, Upper Utility Lift Mooring: 42.05.18 – 2100hrs

The lift locked into its upper mooring. Before her was the command deck hatch. She should get up. She had to report. The captain was waiting for them. Them. Not just her. Reality came rushing back. Yakata yanked herself to her feet with her good arm and gripped the ladder-track for balance. The hatch was open and the deck lights were at standby dim.

Every nerve in her body pricked. The command deck was unmanned. It was never unmanned. Leaning into the ladder, Yakata braced herself. She released her grip with her good hand and reached down into her maintenance kit. Near the bottom, she found the telescoping mirror she'd used earlier. Taking the reflective end carefully between her teeth, she angled the head and drew out the handle as far as it would go. She then edged the tool around the hatch. There were no bodies on the deck, and there were none walking around, either. Not that she could see, anyway.

The lights flared higher as she pulled herself through the hatch. She squinted against the sudden brilliance. It took a moment for her eyes to adjust. Closing the hatch, she keyed the lock with her personal code. Dunn wouldn't corner her again. Her shoulder throbbed in agreement. With a grimace, she settled into the command chair. Multiple warnings lit up the display in front of her. Alerts flashed over nearly every inch of the ship, a confusing dance of flood, fire, and vacuum. Sometimes all three at once in the same compartment. How much of it was real?

Clearing the screen, she prayed nothing would go critical before she could get this sorted out. She ran diagnostics, keying in commands one-handed. Half of the alerts disappeared. Next, she toggled the comm on the console. Nothing. Not even static. She had to try, though.

"Yakata to all crew, report." She set the hail to repeat and went back to diagnostics. It was halfway through and there were no major malfunctions yet. A host of minor ones, but those they could survive. Of course, that assumed the diagnostics system wasn't fried as well.

She then input the command to identify the locations of all on board, just as she had when she looked for Dunn. It took longer this time. The computer spit out multiple conflicting responses. There was no way to tell which one was accurate.

While she waited for diagnostics to complete, Yakata moved to the emergency kit. She selected an analgesic patch. After tearing it open with her teeth, she palmed it and slipped it past the collar of her coverall. It was cool, instantly soothing her battered shoulder. That taken care of, she settled back into the command chair.

Diagnostics was at ninety-five percent. Another alert went off as the logarithm completed. Yakata's eyes moved from the diagnostics display to the main console. It was the proximity warning. It shouldn't have gone off when they were under hyper-drive. She stood and went to the external monitoring station. Nothing appeared on the fore view. Yakata activated the aft cameras. Her finger trembled as she depressed the button. Her vision greyed out one moment, only to telescope into sharp focus the next. Something drifted by the lens out by the drive section, caught in the electromagnetic pocket of e'space surrounding the ship. Several somethings, in fact. Yakata swallowed against the acidic tang climbing her throat. Visions of her father's helmet overwhelmed her, eclipsing the images she didn't want to see. She distanced herself through extreme willpower and zoomed in on the debris.

"...all crew, report."

"Shit!" Yakata yelled as her own voice suddenly called out through both her comm hood and every speaker on the deck. Communications was back. She killed the auto repeat and sent out a fresh hail.

"Command deck to Captain Maberry..."

Her voice trailed off as she tweaked the settings on the monitor. The objects had come into focus. Her eyes slammed closed. But even with them tightly shut she could still see the empty gaze of Captain Maberry staring at her from the vacuum of space.

PERSONAL LOG ENTRY: 42.05.18 – 2230HRS, DUNN, K.

FUCK YOU! I DON'T KNOW WHAT YOU ARE, BUT I KNOW WHAT YOU'RE DOING NOW, SO FUCK YOU! YOU MADE ME HURT HER. I WOULD NEVER HURT HER. SHE IS THE ONLY ONE WHO CARES. WHO STILL MEANS SOMETHING TO ME...

I KNOW YOU CAN ACCESS WHAT I'M WRITING HERE, BECAUSE YOU KNEW HOW TO MESS WITH MY HEAD. WELL ACCESS THIS: YOU WILL NEVER GET ME TO HURT HER AGAIN. YOU WILL NEVER TOUCH HER AGAIN. I WILL DESTROY YOU!

DUTY LOG: 42.05.19 – 1230HRS, YAKATA, U.

REACTOR STATUS – INDETERMINATE;

O_2 LEVELS – FLUCTUATING;

POWER – DATA UNAVAILABLE.

NOTE: SC MCKAY OPERATING UNDER EMERGENCY CONDITIONS. SHIP-WIDE MALFUNCTIONS WORSEN. MEMBER OR MEMBERS OF THE CREW UNSTABLE. CAPTAIN MABERRY; DECEASED, MEANS UNKNOWN, BODY EXPELLED FROM SHIP BY UNIDENTIFIED PERSONNEL. AT LEAST THREE OTHERS LIKEWISE EXPELLED, POSITIVE ID CANNOT BE MADE. CREWMAN CHAPMAN; DECEASED, ACCIDENTAL OR BY DESIGN. CREWMAN DUNN; UNSTABLE, VIOLENT, TEMPORARILY RESTRAINED IN PORT LATERAL AIRLOCK. REMAINDER OF THE CREW;

STATUS UNKNOWN. FIRST OFFICER USHIMI YAKATA ASSUMING COMMAND.

Out of habit, Yakata printed a hard copy of the duty log. Events must always be documented. Not that she expected anyone would ever read this account. As she tore the sheet from the printer, her eyes drifted across the page. She cursed and jerked her hand away. The page drifted to the deck, bold, black letters stared up at her:

THEY'RE ALL DEAD. YOU'RE ALL DEAD. DIE ALREADY, BITCH.

There was the faintest of sounds behind her. She whirled. O'Neal came through the hatch across the command deck, the one leading to the cargo bay and rendezvous station.

She took in the metallurgist's appearance: his coverall was torn, and dark stains across his chest glistened wetly. There was no sign he was the party injured. At his side, his prosthetic arm slowly flexed, as if the motion were unconscious. Yakata met O'Neal's gaze. She did not recognize the man staring back at her. His eyes were cold and hard, alien and bereft of humanity. His expression was neutral; as if she wouldn't notice something else lurked beneath. *There was so much wrong with this picture,* Yakata thought fleetingly.

"You plan to do what you're told?" he asked in a slow drawl, nodding toward the slip of acrylisheet on the floor.

His tone sounded as flat as his expression. Yakata's eyes flickered to the printout.

"I don't take orders from a piece of paper," she growled. "And I sure as hell don't take orders from you."

"We all have to answer to someone."

"Yeah, well the only person I answered to is drifting out by the engines," Yakata spat back at him. "Who do you answer to?" She moved to the side as she spoke, edging toward the hatch.

"You'll meet soon enough." The neutrality was gone. Pure evil crept through O'Neal's voice. He followed her movements like a raptor tracking prey.

Forget that, Yakata told herself. With the line of her body to block the action, she lowered her right hand back into her maintenance kit. Very carefully, she eased out her utility knife, her hand through the wrist strap and the hilt solid in her palm. She depressed the release button on the pommel and the blade silently deployed.

Yakata's muscles rippled beneath her skin. She braced herself, poised to react to whatever move O'Neal made. Her only real option was evasion. If he got a hold of her with that prosthetic, he would crush her before she could even flinch.

As the metallurgist advanced, a tremor went straight through Yakata's body. It took her a moment to realize it wasn't internal. She sucked in a sharp breath. Her gaze flickered away from O'Neal to the main display. Alert icons flashed, one by one. The system was losing power. Within moments they would no longer have enough to sustain hyperdrive. There was a boot dock just behind her and a tether up and to her right. She was going to need one of them shortly.

It would have to be the boot dock; she had too few functioning hands to grab a tether and use the knife. She edged herself closer. Let him think she was afraid of him; that she futilely distanced herself.

She was ready when the bottom dropped out of the universe. The ship shuddered as the electrogravitic drive envelope disintegrated. Simultaneously, she leaned back and jammed her heel into the dock. She was barely secure when there was a pop and a flash as intense as a hundred strobes going off right there in the room. Yakata squeezed her eyes shut just in time. From the heaving sounds, O'Neal had been caught unaware. She opened her eyes as reality righted itself in an orbital orientation. O'Neal floated in an uncontrolled sprawl on the far side of the command console. Around him floated globes of acrid vomit. As he bumped them, they burst into a dozen smaller globes, minus what clung to him. Feebly, his hand reached for the edge of the console.

Yakata grinned. In this state, he was no threat at all.

He groaned, and she laughed. She couldn't help it.

She went somber quickly, though, as hatred sharpened his gaze. The stench of malevolence overpowered the odor of bile. He looked ready to launch at her. Yakata tightened her grip on the utility knife. Let him try. He was a ground-pounder. Space was her element, and this was her ship.

There was a clunk and the manual release on the command deck hatch spun toward open. Yakata froze. Once she'd keyed the lock, even the manual release required her personal code to open the hatch. Only one person onboard had the slightest chance of figuring it out. Dunn.

Confusion infiltrated the evil glint in O'Neal's eye. She watched fury flood his expression as the hatch swung out. The open portal remained empty.

Yakata didn't relax. Now she had to be on her guard on two fronts, and her ex was no rookie in space. He must have been the one to disable the drive system. He certainly had the knowledge.

"Don't just stand there, 'Ta!"

Dunn peered around the edge of the hatch as he snapped at her. The scratch across his face had crusted over. His expression danced between violence and panic. She shifted her grip on the utility knife and turned her body so that her good arm could strike at either O'Neal or Dunn.

From the far side of the command console, O'Neal let out a serpentine hiss. She resisted the urge to turn to stare at him. Dunn represented the more potent threat at the moment.

She watched the muscles of his face clench and twitch in response to the sound O'Neal made. Dunn's breath quickened. The massive spanner he'd used earlier came into view. She braced herself, ready to yank her heel out of the dock the second she knew which direction to propel herself. But his attention wasn't on her. Dunn's eyes locked with O'Neal's. Yakata's gaze flickered from one to the other. Between them, they blocked the only ways out.

"Will you move it before he figures out how to get both of us!"

Yakata jumped, startled as Dunn spoke in rapid Japanese. She'd forgotten he knew her language. It wasn't something they'd used often. They both knew that O'Neal didn't share their knowledge.

The entire crew was required to familiarize themselves with his profile before he came on board. She was surprised Dunn had enough of a grip on himself to use that intel.

"What...and I'm supposed to trust you over him?" She slashed back in the same tongue. "He's not the one who tried to cave in my head!"

"Just move it, 'Ta!" Dunn continued in Japanese. Sweat gleamed on his forehead and his eyes were wild.

Before she could dodge aside, he lunged. His free hand latched onto her belt. She snarled as he jerked her loose from the dock. Yakata gasped with pain, her damaged arm wrenched about by his handling. Her head spun at the sharp, sudden movement. Dunn angled her toward the hatch with practiced ease. At the same time, the hand gripping the spanner swung out, aimed at O'Neal's head.

There was a solid thunk: the sound of metal against flesh. Silence followed. Threat floated thick on the canned air. Yakata shifted her head to look back at O'Neal. His green eyes glowed with malice. She cursed and lost the thought as her quick glance took in his unbloodied head and Dunn's spanner caught by the metallurgist's flesh hand. Some oddly detached part of her brain wondered why he hadn't just grabbed it with the prosthetic.

Her answer was a strangled gasp from Dunn. With no visible effort, O'Neal's cybernetic limb crushed Dunn's wrist, the one holding the spanner.

The sight refocused Yakata's rage in an instant. She tried to wrench away from Karl's grip, throwing herself back as far as his tethering hold allowed to slash at his attacker with her utility knife. The tip sliced through O'Neal's shirt, barely scratching his shoulder. He did not even flinch.

Her curses cut off abruptly as Dunn shook her hard.

"Go! Now!" Karl snapped. Pain glimmered in his eyes, brilliant and jagged. Beneath that, he wordlessly pled with her. She stopped struggling, her brow drawn down in confusion.

Executing an effortless turn, she used the tip of her toe to propel herself off the overhead toward the hatch. She torpedoed through the opening, dropped the utility knife to hang by its strap, and caught the hatch collar with her good hand. Behind her a sick grinding sound filled the command deck.

She pivoted, catching sight of Dunn on his knees, his captured arm bent impossibly high behind his back. She growled and started to return to the command deck. She couldn't leave him to this.

"No! I said go! One of us has to get away...head for the Cans, now!" Despite his obvious pain, he continued speaking in Japanese. Yakata hissed in objection, but she dipped her head in a brief, sharp nod before pivoting around to zip down the main shaft. Behind her, she heard a loud snap as the sick sound of laughter drifted through the hatch. She had to fight the impulse to turn around and tear O'Neal to shreds.

"Yes...do run, little rabbit...I'll be along as soon as I'm done here. Shouldn't take long."

Yakata's blood thickened and her heart froze. O'Neal had just spoken to her in flawless, textbook Japanese.

An agonized scream came from the command deck. It rose sharply before an abrupt end.

Her good arm burned nearly as bad as her injured one. She ignored it and grabbed another rung of the ladder-track, slingshoting herself down the shaft. The echo of Dunn's final scream followed her. It filled her head until she heard nothing else. She tried to force the memory into the fading recesses where it belonged. It resisted.

The flickers of movement were back. The flashes of light behind her, just to the side of her vision. Halfway down the shaft it got to her. Growling deep in her throat, she turned to confront the phantoms that stalked her. A practiced flick of her wrist sent the utility knife back up into her grip and a moment's pressure deployed the blade. Her momentum sent her colliding with the substructure. The impact to her damaged arm sent true sparks across her vision, followed by a grey haze. She blinked it away and cursed.

The shaft behind her was empty. There was nothing behind her, and nowhere anyone might hide. She retracted the knife and let it drift at the end of its strap. With a little more care, she turned and continued to haul herself along, both arms throbbing as she went.

Her comm hood gave a sudden burst of static. Yakata jumped. Another growl filled her throat pulsing against her jaw. She nearly snatched the comm hood off to shred the delicate wiring.

"What the hell are you doing?!"

The unexpected outburst stayed her hand. Dunn. How...? Her gaze snapped to the command deck many stories above her head. She couldn't see him. He must be watching her on the monitors.

"I told you...to get out of here! Get to the Cans...now!" Dunn's voice was thin, strained.

"What happened to O'Neal?"

"Don't know...I passed out. He's not here." Sounds of movement filtered through the comn; rustling, a sharply drawn breath. What might have been a strangled sob...

"Dunn? Dunn!" Yakata's suspicions disintegrated beneath a fresh wave of concern.

"Don't yell, 'Ta." Karl's voice was low and weak. "You're making it hard to think.

"He left me for dead, which means he's after you."

"I don't understand what's going on here," she whispered.

"It's that damn artifact," he snapped back, but his voice quickly faded, slurring and losing focus. "None of this started until we salvaged that thing. It's screwing with our minds. It's screwing with the ship. Somehow it's infiltrated the system...and..." Static disrupted him in sharp bursts. "...anything electronic...nly use manual overr...only. Not malfunc...deliberate."

"The artifact! I have to get the artifact!"

"No!...amnit! Get the hell off this ship. Now!"

Immediately, uncertainty sank firm fingers into her thoughts. She had more reason to doubt Dunn than to trust him. And O'Neal had already proven their attempt at speaking covertly had failed.

"Move!"

No. Perhaps O'Neal left him for dead...or not. Dunn had attacked her once already. She couldn't help but wonder if this was a trap.

She would get her artifact, and then she was getting off this ship. It was foolhardy to continue to the airlocks, though. That's where they expected her to go. Besides, the Cans—as the escape pods were called by any spacer with experience—had precious little reserve, and almost no maneuverability. The distress signal was a joke. She wasn't ditching this ship just to suffocate slowly in space.

Like a swimmer doing laps, Yakata flipped end over end and hauled herself the way she'd come. The pods weren't the only option. There was that payload attached to the forward coupling, the inter-orbital shuttlecraft meant to transport Corporate bigwigs to their facilities surrounding Demeter. Even if O'Neal knew about it, he wouldn't expect her to try and escape that way. Transports were shipped dry, no fuel, no external tanks, and just enough juice to power the maneuvering thrusters and internals. Right now the shuttle was a big, floating box. But—most important for her—that big, floating box contained enough air to support seven adult males for fourteen days, without cracking the reserve tanks. That...and a state-of-the-art distress beacon.

All she had to do was reach it. Yakata renewed her efforts, keeping her eye on the reflectors as she went. No one threatened to come through the hatches ahead of her. As she neared the Temporary Science Lab, she again glanced both ways down the shaft.

Wherever O'Neal had gone, he wasn't stalking her.

Yakata opened the compartment and dove inside. She thanked God that the drive had not reengaged. The only blessing in this whole thing: weightlessness certainly made it easy to get around. Not to mention the obelisk would have been a dead weight if the ship were still under gravity.

Lights flared as Yakata slipped into the section where the artifact was stored. Immediately she noticed the door to the locker hung open, and nothing remained inside.

"No!" Yakata hissed with rage. She looked around, her gaze darting frantically, as if the obelisk might be sitting right in front of her. But it was useless. It was gone. She slammed the locker door and whirled, her anger taking over. The spectrometer still sat affixed to the table. It mocked her. She'd known O'Neal was out to screw her over. Her good hand snapped out, denting the housing of his costly machine. She let it fly again. It felt good. She took aim once more, until a reflection in the battered metal caught her eye.

O'Neal! She dove away from his raised fists, certain that any moment she would feel the crushing blow from his prosthetic. None fell. She twisted in midair, fighting to control her motions, to palm her knife and deploy the blade.

As she came to rest against the far bulkhead, Yakata felt a ripple of laughter seize her throat.

"What the hell?" she murmured aloud. The room was empty. No O'Neal hovered, ready to pummel her to pulp. Yet...

Yakata gripped her knife tighter and propelled herself toward the spectrometer. Had she truly lost it? Or was this proof of the sinister force Dunn claimed now possessed the ship? She tapped the dented surface with the tip of her utility knife. Tapped it right over the reflection of O'Neal. The micro image flinched back. Yakata giggled. It sounded jagged.

That was it then: she'd gone over the edge. She giggled again and chased the figmentary O'Neal around the spectrometer with rapid taps of her utility knife. She laughed full out and tasted salt drip over the rim of her lip onto her tongue. A sob slipped out next. The knife drifted down to its strap and she rested a gentle hand against the reflection.

"I'm sorry...I'm so sorry..."

She brought her face right up near the metal, noticing the terror on that tiny man's face. He wasn't looking at her, though; his gaze stared off into the room. It took her a moment to realize there were now two O'Neals trapped in the metal. Perhaps it was an accumulative thing: the longer she stared the more the image would multiply. Her next giggle bordered on a wail.

That was when the *ching* of flexing metal reached her ears. Her eyes went wide. She leaned against the machine. Clarity seeped back into her own reflection. The memory of the last time she and O'Neal had been in this room came to her. He'd taken the artifact out of the spectrometer and gone into painful convulsions. Her gaze snapped to the tiny O'Neal with the hazel eyes, somehow trapped within his own machine while something went around in his body. He gave the slightest nod. "I am sorry," she whispered as she snaked her hand around the housing.

With a mighty heave, she flung the machine at the O'Neal creeping up behind her, the one with something alien peering out of stormy green eyes.

Power couplings snapped. Metal collided with metal in a satisfying crunch. The creature's roar deafened her.

As she rocketed past, aiming for the hatch, she spared half a glance for her would-be attacker. The spectrometer drifted away from him. Massive bruises shadowed O'Neal's already dark shoulder. The prosthetic attached to it was crumpled, but the fingers flexed, if somewhat haltingly.

Her aim was off. She'd meant to cave in his head.

There was an odd gleam in O'Neal's eye as he locked gazes with her. She jerked her eyes away and maneuvered out of arm's reach.

She was nearly clear when he lurched up. His flesh hand shot out and grabbed her ankle. Screaming with rage, she flicked her wrist and palmed the dangling utility knife, the blade still deployed. She lashed out. The edge bit deep into the back of his hand.

She jerked the knife free and kicked out with her unfettered foot at O'Neal's still firm and bloodied grip on her ankle. He laughed up at her. The trapped O'Neal pounded furiously from the far side of his reflection; the evil one raised his battered prosthetic and caressed her calf with deceptive gentleness.

Frantic, Yakata tried to yank her foot free. She succeeded only in drawing him closer. Again the prosthetic stroked her leg, this time higher.

"Shh...it'll be okay..." he mocked.

Her vision went dark and flat. Nothing had depth or shading. Nothing was as crisply clear as his grip on her leg. Nothing mattered more than freeing herself from that hold. Without a second thought, she brought her knife around again and impaled O'Neal's hand...

...straight through to her ankle. More blood filled the room.

"Augh!"

O'Neal laughed over her scream as he tugged his hand away from the blade, bisecting his own flesh. The damage did nothing to hinder his movements. But for her, the motion sent shafts of breath-stopping pain shooting from her foot to the top of her head. The knife remained lodged in the muscle just above the ankle.

"Bad girl...you were supposed to head for the Cans."

Yakata whimpered. Clenching her teeth, she yanked out the blade, sending pearls of blood spinning through the bay. The strap went back over her wrist. The hilt locked in her grip. Again armed, she kicked off toward the hatch.

From just inside the room, O'Neal's laughter stole her breath. She waited for him to haul her back. She could already feel his fingers locked around her. Not again! She sent herself rocketing forward with reckless force. Her body careened off the interior walls. She slammed against the hatch collar with her bad shoulder. The injured foot snagged on the door. Agony nearly crippled her as her vision clouded and a buzz filled her ears.

It wasn't enough to drown out O'Neal as he called after her. "Run, little rabbit, run...it's so much fun to catch you."

Despite O'Neal's taunt, there were no sounds of pursuit. She had no illusion it would remain that way. Tumbling into the main shaft, Yakata planted her good foot against the track and shoved off, bulleting toward the nose of the ship. She cursed at the lights. Some sections activated as she passed, others went out, plunging her into darkness. She ignored it. After all her years on this ship, a little darkness wasn't going to screw her up.

As she neared the command deck there was a faint green ambient glow, like that given off by digital displays in the dark. It was impossible to make out if anyone was there. O'Neal was somewhere behind her, but what happened to Dunn? Intense sorrow gripped her heart as she remembered the last time she saw him. Yakata forced it away. He was either dead, or a danger to her.

Cautiously, she eased past the command hatch, keeping to the far side of the shaft. It was slow going, but she made it to the staging bay two levels up without incident. A glance behind her revealed no obvious motion, but her nerves vibrated with tension.

She turned back to the open hatch of the staging bay. The mechanism to seal the two-meter wide opening could close in less than thirty seconds. She released the knife and reached into her pouch for a spanner, wedging it into the grating where the retractable hatch was housed. It wouldn't hold long, but should another...malfunction occur, the obstruction would give her a little extra time to get clear.

Reaching just past the opening, she felt around for a tether bar to haul herself through. Something brushed against her hand in the darkness. She jerked back and palmed the knife, bracing herself for an attack. A whisper of sound taunted her ears. Her grip on the knife tightened even more, but nothing else came at her out of the dark. Yakata breathed out a growl.

Fine, she thought. *I'll do it the hard way.* She flung herself through the hatch, rocketing past the opening and deep into the bay, her body angled to intersect with the lift track. Instead, she collided with something soft and yielding. It was impossible not to scream as arms came around to encircle her.

No! She would not be caught so easily! Yakata brought up her knife and thrust brutally into the one blocking her way.

"'Ta..." The whisper was faint, and right by her ear. Yakata moaned and her knife hand jerked back. Warm globules bounced against her skin as the blade did more damage coming out than going in. The pinpoints of warmth sent her trembling.

No! Oh, God, no! Please no! Yakata's thoughts were frantic. She released the knife as if it were a contagion. Her now-empty hand scrambled around in her maintenance pouch as the knife bobbed on its strap. *Where was it? Where, damnit?* She forgot all about escape as she searched for her spare light among the jumbled tools. As her hand wrapped around it, and she depressed the button, a sudden clang from the direction of the hatch startled her. She fumbled the light. It made eerie arcs as it spun in the darkened bay, revealing small slices of her surroundings. Her gasp echoed through the compartment as the rotating beam briefly illuminated a blood-coated hand. Yakata lunged for the maintenance light. Before she could bring the beam around, there was a deep, rumbling chuckle behind her. She whirled and the main lights flared to life in the bay. She flinched and squinted against the sudden brilliance.

"My...and haven't you been busy?" O'Neal rested against the lift track, his arms crossed over his chest as he watched her. She noticed his gaze sweep the chamber. He frowned faintly as he looked right, but he made no move toward her or the room.

The last thing she should do was take her eyes off him. The impulse, however, was irresistible. Yakata pivoted until she could see the whole of the bay.

The blood rushed from her head. She barely heard O'Neal's malicious laughter. Around her floated three bodies. Her un-accounted-for crewmen...She immediately recognized the one to the right as Dunn, much bloodier, but still clearly him. The closest to her, however, was John Pittman. From his gut streamed a trail of ruby-red bubbles.

She was overcome by the urge to fling the utility knife from her, only that would have cut her probability of survival down even lower. It was an effort to tug her eyes away, to get past the horror. She told herself he was already dead. Beyond Pittman floated Anita Suarez, her expression softer, more feminine in death than it had ever been in life. Old spacer that she was, she looked like a frightened child now. A frightened child frozen in intense and unbearable pain.

Yakata refused to look more closely at Dunn.

She cursed and turned on O'Neal once more, her knife in her hand, though she didn't remember flicking it up. O'Neal continued to laugh.

"'Ta...no...."

Again, the bodiless whisper by her ear. No...from her comm hood! Only Dunn ever call her 'Ta. She glanced sideways, trying to catch the subtle motion breathing alone would have caused. It was so hard to tell at this angle.

"Damn it, 'Ta, come...get this thing..." The strained whisper was no product of her imagination. He 'drifted' ever so slightly; just enough to reveal the outline of a line-gun hidden in the curve of his body. Behind him she could see the half-open storage locker the tool had come from.

Without another thought, she braced both legs against the wall. Pain rippled from her ankle, but she needed equal force to keep herself headed straight as she launched herself forward. O'Neal arrowed toward Dunn, as well, but Yakata was closer.

Grasping the gun and using her momentum to pivot the rest of her mass, she braced the improvised weapon against her body and jerked the release.

There was a *whoosh* and a *thud*. O'Neal went rocketing across the bay toward the opposite wall. His head slammed into the hull and then the only motion was his body recoiling from the impact.

Numbness set in. *Could that be it? Was it that simple?* she thought as she drifted where she was, the gun still gripped in her hand. Beside her, Dunn moaned and it barely reached where her psyche had retreated.

The steady tug on the rope, though...that went right to her nerve centers.

"Oh, shit!" She let go of the line-gun and wrapped her good hand in Dunn's vest.

"N-no...you have to survive," he murmured, batting away her hand. "Can't do that hauling my ass behind you."

"Bullshit!" she growled. "You made it this far, I'm not leaving you here to die."

"I'm...I'm d-dead, either way."

She ignored his failing whisper, and pushed off, sending them past the bodies. Her mind shut down as she did so, focused on one goal: freedom. Nothing existed but the nose dock of the *McKay* and the payload it led to.

And suddenly, they were there.

She let go of Dunn's vest to work the manual release. The hatch clanged open and she reached for Dunn once more. He gripped her hand back. He trembled violently. She turned to look at him, to gauge how much distress he was in.

"No!" she shouted, as she spied O'Neal past Dunn's shoulder, raising the retracted line-gun. But it was too late. She felt the impact as the hook embedded itself in Karl's back. "No...no..." she sobbed. Not Dunn. Not when she... "No...I l-love you! No!"

Tears streamed down her face as she watched the awareness fade from his eyes. *No.* But this protest was silent, weak. *Does it matter now,* she wondered, *if I get away?* But the tug of the line decided her. She roared with rage and yanked back. O'Neal and whatever rode him would not have Dunn.

She brought up her utility knife and severed the line. Grabbing Karl's vest, she tugged him through the forward airlock. He bobbed behind her as she cycled the hatch. Yakata was numb as she took them through the yacht access. She gave him a gentle nudge to send him drifting deeper into the cabin as her hand danced automatically through the manual release sequence for the docking ring.

As they separated from the *McKay,* she could swear she heard the ghost of O'Neal's laughter.

She dropped into the command chair of the luxury yacht, barely noticing the sensual caress of fine doeskin leather. Her only concern was powering up the systems. Lighting and atmospherics engaged, followed by the exterior cameras.

The numbness faded as she realized how near Demeter they were. There was hope of rescue. A solid chance for survival. Her hand hovered over the distress beacon, but drew back, leaving the unit inactivated. Why bother? Dunn was gone.

"No...you must survive."

Yakata shivered as Dunn's earlier words whispered through her thoughts. Clenching her eyes against the heartache, she brought her hand back and slammed it down on the distress beacon button.

Rescue would come now. And she would have to go on. Alone.

As that realization hit her, she watched the *McKay* fire its engines. She deftly manipulated the contoured joystick controlling the external camera, panning it in the ship's wake.

What is he up to now? she wondered, unable to turn away. The *McKay* angled further to the left and the display in front of her blazed fiercely, blinding her a moment. The system adjusted the filters until the brilliant sun was no more than a distant, glowing disk marred only by a rapidly diminishing black speck.

"Enjoying the show, Ms. Ushimi?"

Yakata jerked as O'Neal's voice came over the yacht's speakers. She cursed herself for forgetting to disengage the remote sensors connecting the two ships.

"Why?" she hissed.

"Where's the terror," he purred, "if there's no one left to know exactly how fucked you all are?

"Oh yes, and thanks for the ride."

As his words faded, the yacht's lights flickered out, plunging Yakata into darkness. She fumbled with the control panel, frantically trying to reengage them, to no avail. Her only illumination was the display in front of her.

She couldn't hold back a whimper. She was no longer comfortable with the dark. O'Neal's disembodied laugh wrapped around her just before he closed the link. She was so shocked it took a moment for her to realize the *McKay's* hyperdrive had engaged.

Horrified, she watched the ship's graceful arc; the shimmer of its electrogravitic drive envelope mesmerized her. Yakata held her breath. She could still see the glittering trail streaming behind the transport, but knew it had, in fact, already plunged into the sun. Eight minutes later, the sunlight contracted, the glowing ball getting smaller and smaller.

O'Neal's voice echoed in her head. An old memory from when he had still been himself and the spectrometer had fed them an impossible reading on the obelisk: *It's as if the artifact absorbed the light.*

She shuddered and watched as the star died, its fire eaten up by an ancient evil no larger than her head.

Yakata found herself in complete darkness with her dead.

Dunn. The spaced crew. In her panicked mind, she pictured each of them in a mask of her father's face.

Her breath came in rapid huffs and her body shook until she had to grip the console to remain in the chair.

How long before we all die? she thought, staring in the direction of Demeter, an entire planet suddenly and inexplicably plunged into bitter-cold darkness.

The comm hood crackled and Yakata's heart seized.

"Yummy," O'Neal's voice whispered malevolently in her ear. "Want to come get us? We'll do dessert..."

Yakata screamed.

This is precisely the type of story C.J. would have written, with quirk and danger and deep concepts all intertwined.

The Editors

The seed for "Finder" came from a short story that I never finished called "Knocking Down Walls" about a character who found unusual, strange, and sometimes supernatural items, The main character, Tony was someone who started out normal and was changed so that his view of the world had to broaden enough to accept the inexplicable. I won't say that C.J. Henderson's The Things That Are Not There and Teddy London's own revelation about the nature of the strange directly influenced me; but I felt there was a definite parallel in the two characters. So when I was asked to write a story for the anthology, Tony Reid was definitely the right choice.

Jeff Young

Finder

Jeff Young

JUST PAY ME. SIMPLE, STRAIGHTFORWARD PAYMENT always works perfectly. When the subject of favors given or owed comes up, life becomes complicated — especially when the owed party is dead.

My knees were up against the back of the seat in front of me partially covering a sticker with the name C.J. Henderson on it. I was attempting to level out the surface of my tablet so I could type as Spindle drove the cab.

"Reid, yo Reid, ya listenin'" Spindle shouted over the music. "I'm spinning at Hell No Kitty tonight, you should check it out. Trisia says you're usually there anyway. I just got some sick tracks." He drove like he DJ'ed, way more fingertips on the wheel instead of the traditional ten and two hold. Sometimes it felt like he was braking in time to the dubstep blaring over the speakers. "I'll probably be there. Keep all the wheels on the pavement." I went to the bar for totally different reasons, although Trisia's being there was definitely a bonus.

I tried once again to consider Abramowitz's email, but couldn't. One of my friends was dead, his current girlfriend missing, and the whole debacle couldn't have happened to a nicer guy. No, really, he really was the nicest guy I knew, that meant that the level of cutthroats, liars, and people who shouldn't be trusted with anything more dangerous than a spork in my circle of "friends" had just risen exponentially. Now wasn't the time to take on another client but I couldn't ignore this email either.

I wanted to have a look at Prester's place before I started thinking about anything else. So I drew my fingers together on the surface of the tablet and the email folded up and slid off to one side. As I tucked the tablet back into my pant's cargo pocket, I caught a brief flash of my reflection. My blond stubble was one step from being bald. *Come on*, I thought, *time to focus*. Instead I looked out the window at the passing city blocks and tried not to think too hard about Prester.

I was going to Prester's to see what I could *find*. That's what I did or mostly what people paid me for, finding objects or answers. I had a knack. It wasn't something I was born with; amusingly enough it found me. I'd done a favor for an unknown entity high enough up in the food chain of either the camp of ethereal goodness or downright demonic naughtiness a favor and they changed my nature, giving me this little gift. Then just to be truly ironic, this unknown benefactor took away my memory of what I did to put them in my debt, making that knowledge the one thing I can't *find*.

Everything else just comes to me unbidden. An uncle's hidden bank account in the Caymans, a child given up for adoption, or perhaps something even a little more obscure like Babe Ruth's favorite bat. That's really where my talent lay, finding the truly unusual. After all, some of these items are hard to find for a very, very good reason. It took awhile to realize it but this talent of mine could actually pay my way in the world. Sometimes it took a great deal of work and risk. That would be why I am not so fond of favors.

On the other hand, I owed Prester. More than once Simon Prester had been there when I was down and out before I'd acquired my "talent". He'd asked only one thing in return, "If and when I shuffle off this mortal coil, just check in on what was important to me. I hate to leave things unfinished." So I was heading over to his self-made farm to follow through on that promise.

The incident report I'd intercepted from the local PD said that his skull was fractured in several places but the broken neck was what killed him. Forensics determined he'd been thrown against the wall, evidenced by the star pattern of broken plaster at the point of impact and pieces found in his hair. The boot that kicked him in the head, snapping his neck while he lay on the floor left a partial bloody footprint before its owner wiped it off on the area rug.

Spindle fishtailed the cab to a showy stop, throwing cinders and gravel into the air, generating small dust devils. I opened the door and shoved a debit card through the window at him. He slid it quickly before launching it back over his shoulder at me. We've played this game plenty of times before, so I caught it and stowed it away without looking.

I ducked as more gravel flew up when Spindle drove off. In front of me was a patch of vegetables and small fruit trees that would have looked more at home miles beyond the outskirts of the city. I walked the paths between the garden beds, framed in cinderblocks, toward the small split-level rancher. The back of the property sloped down in terraces toward the immense warehouse that loomed over the farm, placing the front door on the second floor. In China, these houses were known as "nail homes". The owner was so stubborn that roads, apartment complexes, and factories were simply built around the offending property instead of demolishing it. Prester's father had been that stubborn and his son inherited not only the property but also the same trait.

Ordinarily there would have been people about. But I had a feeling that the yellow police tape across the doorway put them off. I didn't let it stop me. Lifting it up, I walked in like I owned the place. His house hadn't been ransacked, so the police were not leaning toward a robbery. I knew Prester well enough to believe he had nothing worth stealing. In fact, he was more likely to give things away including the produce from his farm. He'd reclaimed the land from the grounds of the failed businesses in an abandoned section of the city. When the government turned off the electricity, Prester set up his own windmill and waterwheel. When the others joined him, he showed them how to set up their own plots. When the farm began generating enough produce he'd bought solar panels to hang on the roofs of the abandoned warehouses. He gave up the grid in the middle of the grid. But someone ended all of that, and I was going to find out who. I wasn't going to forget my promise. I also knew I'd have to find Prester's girl, Ione. Finding people was always harder. They tended to up and move when you least expected it.

I was at a loss for a motive for Prester's death; I stood there staring at the starred pattern on the wall in the living room. Someone big had thrown him against that wall. He'd flown over an end table, struck the wall, and fallen to the left leaving the table standing. Small drops of blood rayed out from the center of the impact. That was when I noticed the blood spatter that stood out from the others. It was a streak like a brush stroke, which grew thinner at its terminus pointing downward. That was when my talent kicked in. I was already crouching down looking at the underside of the table. My eyes caught the one tiny spot of blood on the carpet that was easy to disregard as a fallen drop. My fingers slid along underneath until they found something. It was an earring. That's how my talent works. I find myself doing what it takes to find my target without any thought of my own.

The diamond in the earring winked at me. I don't know a whole lot about jewelry but it struck me that the setting was pretty unusual. There were markings etched into the metal that were just visible around the stone. I could see how the police could have missed it in their search. The earring shot off of Prester's head on impact. It slid down the wall bouncing off of the floor coming to rest adhered to the underside of the end table. I thought about Prester and remembered he'd always worn a small golden hoop. This was new. I felt a sudden twitch between my shoulder blades. I'd found what I was looking for, but what did it mean?

Perhaps, a visit to Abramowitz would be in order, after all he was a jeweler and I was putting off dealing with his email. But before that, I took a look around the rest of the house. There was a small kitchen, two bedrooms, a bath, a living room, and a deck out back just visible through a pair of French doors. I started with Prester's desk in the larger of the two bedrooms. There was a stack of flyers for a benefit on the left hand side. Picking one up, I glanced at it briefly. "Save C.J. Henderson" was printed in large letters across the top. There were about 20 of them. I thought the name sounded familiar. Then I recalled reading one of his Teddy London books.

The sound of the front door opening echoed through the house and I froze. Footsteps. I threw down the papers and rushed toward the rear of the house. I slid open the French doors in the back, ducked under the rail of the deck and over the side. I grabbed a hold of the edge behind a large planter and swung kicking in the air above the concrete slab of the carport below. I hung there for several minutes as the other visitor came outside. Heavy footsteps went back and forth before finally going back into the house.

A loud bang and the sound of smashing glass came through the open French door. Now that the crime scene work was done, apparently Prester's unwelcome visitor felt no need to be subtle. As the noise continued, I dropped down to the ground next to Prester's truck. It didn't take me long to find the keys. I got it started and drove away as fast as I could, looking over my shoulder repeatedly. I hoped whoever was tossing Prester's house was making enough noise that he hadn't heard the truck. If I was really lucky I wouldn't have to explain to the police why I had borrowed it.

I drove through alleyways that ran between the abandoned factories fast enough that their brick walls became a blur. I looped back around, parking the truck out of sight of the house. Slowly I worked my way through the gardens until I could see the front yard. I needed to be able to see just who was tearing up Prester's home. Pulling my little GoPro camera out my jacket pocket, I set it up so it viewed the house. Hiding behind a large, terra cotta planter I slid my tablet out of my cargo pocket, synced with the camera and zoomed in on the house. There was a large black SUV in front, I adjusted the focus until I could see the license plate and snapped a picture. A moment later the driver came out and from his size, I was fairly certain I was not only looking at who ransacked Prester's house but possibly his attacker. I snapped as many shots as I could, saving them in a file marked "Musclehead". He was tall and broad-shouldered with olive skin and thick, heavy black brows. Black gloves covered his hands. When he turned I thought I saw something on his neck. After a bit of zooming in I found a small tattoo behind his left ear. *Aleph*, I realized looking at the image again recognizing the Arabic letter. I reached into my pocket and pulled out the earring—there was a curling mark at the edge of the setting. It could be more Arabic. It was definitely past time to go visit Abramowitz. I sent the jeweler an email to let him know I was stopping by. I also attached several pictures of the earring to the message.

After parking Prester's truck several blocks away from the jeweler's brownstone, I sat in the vehicle for several moments doing some work on the tablet. I sent the pictures via an anonymous server to the police station for identification; the bot resident in their system would send the images my way when the task was done. Yes, it was good to have hacker friends sometimes. Sliding the tablet back into my pocket, I started down the alleyway.

After letting the bronze doorknocker drop, I shoved my hands into my jacket. March in the city was still cold and the wind howled through the buildings, scudding the clouds along overhead making them long, thin, and wispy. The air had a burnt scent to it and when David Abramowitz opened the door I was glad to step inside. His gray hair exploded from his head and chin almost like a collar, framing yellowed glasses that were large enough to be goggles. Shoulders slumped; he turned to lead me along the long hallway away from the foyer and down a series of steps to his workshop. Various rings and other pieces of jewelry were scattered about on the low table. He picked them up, carefully transferring them to nearby shelves so that we would have room to use the surface. David gestured toward a wooden chair upholstered in red leather and then sat across from me. Before saying anything, he pulled out a letter and a torn envelope and passed them over.

"It's my son," he said, as I quickly scanned over the note.

"Isn't he away at college?" I asked, continuing to read.

"That's just it. Someone is threatening to give certain evidence to the security department at school implicating him in drug trafficking. Isaac isn't perfect, but he would never do anything like that. They are blackmailing me. I want to you to find out who would do something like this."

I looked over the paper once I'd read it through, turning it over in my hands. It was heavier than typical grade and when I held it up to the light I was surprised to find a familiar Arabic letter watermarked in the lower corner. "Do you recognize this?" I asked Abramowitz, indicating the *aleph.*

His sharp intake of breath was all response I needed. He looked away.

"Come on, David, you need my help, now I need yours. What does it mean?"

"Nothing good," he retorted sharply and looked me hard in the eye. "Let me see the diamond you asked about."

Not sure about the sudden shift in focus, I handed over Prester's earring. David grunted once and reached behind him for a jeweler's loupe. Peering at the diamond and its setting he pursed his lips and sucked on his teeth. He pulled out a pair of needle-nosed pliers and gently bent up all of the tines holding the diamond in the setting. Then with a sharp intake of breath, he quickly bent down two of the tines once again. "Leave this with me," David said, pulling the loupe from his eye.

"You know I can't do that any more than I can forget what you've told me about Isaac," I replied, reaching for the diamond.

David closed his hand and for a brief moment we struggled for the stone. "If I give them this they just might let him go without doing anything," David coughed out, his breath coming in hoarse gasps.

Instead of trying to pry his fingers apart, I closed mine about his, "They *who*, David?"

He wouldn't meet my gaze and we stood there a moment until a sudden gust of wind struck the house. Then he dropped the diamond and turned away from me. As I bent to pick it up David answered. "They are the Sons of Aleph, a splinter group of Hezbollah, still intent on causing unrest in the Middle East. Still intent on causing trouble here."

When I stood up with the diamond in my hand, David swung back around and pointed at the earring. "And that is what they want me to do. Did you see the setting on the earring? It is engraved with the sacred texts to bind the diamond in place. I have only heard of one such instance where this was done. My grandfather was given the diamond the Tear of El Ahraaz to cut into smaller stones. He was paid handsomely to set each stone with words of binding. Then each stone was scattered around the world where they would never again be joined together. The Sons of Aleph want me to unset the stones that they have because they know that only one of my family can undo what my grandfather bound."

Looking down at the earring, I thought about what he'd said. It was possible that there might be a buyer interested in the historic value of the pieces of the Tear of El Ahraaz who might pay handsomely and therefore fund the Sons of Aleph. Just as possible was the unfortunate fact that the diamond initially had some otherworldly power that the Sons were seeking. It also made sense that the Sons of Aleph were the ones responsible for Prester's death. I closed my fingers around the earring. It didn't matter where they hid, I was going to find them and drag them kicking and screaming into the cold light of day.

"Here's what you'll do, David. You'll tell them that you'll do what they ask and that you know who has another one of the diamonds. You can give them this number." I pulled out a business card and handed it to him. "Hopefully, I can make sure that the police or Homeland Security find them first. But you'll be doing enough that Isaac should be off the hook one way or another."

"Reid, I don't know what to say. I just can't let anything happen to Isaac. He is all I have since his mother passed away."

"David, I understand. But more importantly, do you? We'll work this out, just do your part. Now I'd best be going."

Standing in the doorway, I looked back at David, who looked even older and more shrunken than before. Then I turned away and stepped out into the street. I used my talent to find who was watching me but it turned out that the only one that was interested was a squirrel hanging on the side of tree half a block away. That would have to be good enough for now. I made my way back to Prester's truck and then on to the Hell No Kitty Bar.

When I walked in, Trisia slid a sixteen-year old single malt across the bar until it came to rest two inches from the end. As I walked up to her I wondered briefly how long she'd practiced that trick. She wiped her hands off on a plaid towel and then reached out, put both of them on either side of my face, and pulled me in to kiss me on the cheek. Her thick blonde hair was gathered into long braids that cascaded down her back, rustling as she moved.

"Hey, Ice Maiden," I said.

She threw me a knowing smile and cocked her hip to one side. "Did you find my keys yet?"

I pointed at the drink shaker at the end of the bar and raised an eyebrow. We always play this game.

She swayed over to pick up her keys and gestured toward the first booth. It was early and the bar only had a few patrons. She knew I liked to sit and watch the crowd rather than drink and talk. I slid across the wooden bench and leaned against the back wall letting the murmur of the bar drift over me. Most people need a quiet place to think. Me, I'm the opposite. I find patterns in odd places. So I need something like a background hum, a *susurrus*, a tintinnabulation or, in this case, half-heard conversations to spark my talent. Anyone who watches shooting stars will tell you that you see more when you relax your eyes and don't try to focus. In this case I was looking for stray diamonds.

Sherlock Holmes had his violin and Nero Wolfe had his orchids. Me, I have a seedy bar with a goddess for a barmaid. Sipping the scotch, I thought about diamonds, about the letter *aleph*, and the mysterious Tear of El Ahraaz. Poking at my tablet brought up a few legends about El Ahraaz including the one where the ancient king captured a djinni. El Ahraaz's wish was to live forever and the djinni's answer was to transform the king into one of his own kind and claim his servitude. From thereafter the king did all of the djinni's tasks and the other retired in peace. What that had to do with the diamonds I couldn't say.

The gems were, on the other hand, something that could be tracked. The jeweler who worked with them logged the style of their cut and their weight in carats. They had a paper trail that could be followed, even by the Sons. Then the information would be turned over to Musclehead for pick up.

Smooth and golden on my tongue, the scotch distracted me from my research. I put my hands down on the table and pushed the tablet away. Then I listened. Snatches of conversations drifted in and out. I closed my eyes. I wasn't really hearing words now, just sounds. Free-associated images drifted through my mind. I reached into my pocket and pulled out the diamond, clenching it in my right hand. Suddenly, a very clear image came to me of Abramowitz clearing away the diamonds from his worktable. There were two rings and a broach. I focused on the image, looking at the diamonds. My talent kicked in and the diamonds grew closer until they appeared to be right under my eyes, each bearing the same brilliance and cut as the one in my hand. David was already at work unseating the stones. He was only hoping I could find the Sons of Aleph first. I felt my talent starting to pull on me — to draw me back to Abramowitz. Find him and I would find the Sons of Aleph.

I took the scotch and swallowed the rest in one gulp. It really was a crime to do that, but I needed to go. I stopped and kissed Trisia on the cheek before I strode toward the door.

"Keep safe, Reid, and come back tomorrow," she said, then snapped me on the ass with her towel before returning to polishing glasses.

As I rounded the corner to head to Prester's truck I nearly ran over two men wearing knit hats and a suspended pail like a Salvation Army collection drum. The larger, Italian-looking man — "Rocky" according to the stitching on his hat — wore a sandwich-sign that said "Save C.J. Henderson" in large black letters. The other, a slender Asian man bearing the knitted moniker of "Noodles", rang a somewhat discordant bell. I emptied my pockets into the pail and just managed not to toss the diamond in with all of my loose change. That would be just what I needed now. The clangor of the bell followed me down the street until I came up to Prester's truck.

Abramowitz's door stood open and my talent prodded me to enter, but I was being cautious. Instead I went around the block and peered through the back window. Hands around my face, I looked deep into the house but couldn't find anything amiss. That was until I had a gun shoved into the back of my head and I realized I should listen to my gift in the future. My hands came away from the window and went up into the air, as my arm was grasped to spin me around.

Prester's girlfriend leveled the gun at my face. I couldn't help but notice Ione's rock-solid grip. The wind brushed her cheek-length dark hair back and forth. Her hard eyes locked on mine and the coldness there made me swallow uncomfortably. I had to admit I'd never really liked her when I first met her but I didn't want to judge Prester's choices. I'd found ways to give Ione the benefit of the doubt instead of trying to find what she was really up to. If she was involved with the Sons of Aleph, she'd gotten Prester killed and I was going to make her pay for that.

"I know how you work, so no funny stuff," Ione said, gesturing toward the alleyway with the gun.

I looked at her a moment. "Do the bad guys always talk like that? 'Funny stuff'? Really?"

She cracked me on the jaw with the gun then returned her aim to my face, unwavering.

Trisia always said that one day my mouth might get me killed. Perhaps today wasn't the day to prove her right. "Okay, okay. You got the gun. What do you want?"

"That's easy. I want you to find the rest of the diamonds." Ione's grin was the only twitchy part about her.

"They're in the house." The moment I said that, my talent realized the statement wasn't true. It whipped me around, like a weather vane, to point toward the center of the city. I stood there for a second hoping Ione wasn't going to shoot me for not staying still.

But apparently she meant what she said; she knew what was going to happen with my talent. She gestured me ahead of her, then tucked the hand with the gun into her windbreaker pocket, but still obviously pointed at me. "I'll take that as a 'no' then. Lead on, McDuff."

"It's actually 'Lay on McDuff'." One quick glance at her eyes convinced my that my life expectancy would increase if I just shut up. But then that really wasn't me. "So how's working for the Sons of Aleph going for you so far?"

"Sons of Assholes is closer," was her quick response. "It's amazing Homeland Security hasn't locked up every one of them the way they bumble around. It's purely a monetary arrangement."

"And how did that arrangement go when it came to Prester?"

Her footsteps stopped behind me. I looked over my shoulder and turned part of the way around. Ione was looking down at the ground.

"It was all so stupid. Prester told me about your talent. I had the one diamond, what I really needed was more. I gave him the one in the hope he would ask you to find its mate and then you'd just find all of them. How did I know the stupid bastard would stick it in his own ear instead? How could I know that the Sons wouldn't wait, that they would find him, that they would ..." She broke off in a brief sob. Then her head lifted and the look she gave me was one of pure hate. "And now we're going to finish this and then I'm going to finish them. Get moving, Reid. Find me the diamonds and you'll find me those sons of bitches."

The wind kicked through the litter, scattering leaves and paper cups against our legs as we moved along the side streets. I stopped and looked up at the clouds overhead. They'd turned heavy, black shadows crawling along their undersides. There was a storm on the way. Across the street was a large mural painted on the brick wall. Again huge letters proclaimed "Save C.J. Henderson". A round, bewhiskered face smiled benevolently down on me and I wondered if anyone would be saving me any time soon.

"Come on," urged Ione.

My talent pulled us over several streets and then headed us toward Market Street. I ignored Ione's noise of consternation.

Sometimes the ability gets like this. If I'm finding something really big it's almost like an unavoidable attraction. I'm pulled faster and faster to the inevitable conclusion. That's when I really see *finding* for what it is. It is a power, a power that can rearrange circumstance to its favor. There is no such thing as serendipity. It may feel like it, but rather it's like fate suddenly has a downhill slope. Everything gravitates to the conclusion and I have to really wonder over and over, is the end result good or evil?

We were about three blocks away from Market Street when I heard a disturbance coming from the intersection. It was time to start distracting Ione. If I wanted to get away, I'd need her off balance — especially since my value dropped to nil once she got the diamonds.

"So what do you know about djinn?" I asked.

"More than you do, Reid. Keep walking."

"Hey, I haven't stopped. Just asking."

"Bet you don't know about the heart of the djinni, do you, Reid?"

I suspected I could find out, but my talent was already encouraging me to shut up and keep walking toward the diamonds.

"Djinn are spirits of wind and fire from the Middle East. Spirits that spin so hot and so fast—"

"That their centers turn carbon into diamonds," I finished for her. The truth unfolded for me in rather nasty clarity and suddenly I was incredibly sure that neither Ione nor the Sons of Aleph should ever get their hands on the parts necessary to reanimate a djinni. If you were a terrorist looking for a weapon capable of mass destruction, easily portable and nearly undetectable, a djinni in the form of a handful of cut diamonds would be tough to beat.

We turned the last corner and I saw two things before Ione did. A parade completely filled Market Street with floats and bands and people marching. Musclehead stood out on the sidelines. I started to run about the same instant that he launched himself into the parade. We were both heading toward a missing diamond. I was damn certain the others were in his pocket from the pull dragging me toward him.

Ione only had enough time to draw a breath and for that I was glad. Already I was three loping paces ahead of her. The end of the alleyway loomed before us and then I was running into the by-standers, forcing my way out into the street. I took an elbow in the ribs, backed away from a swing at my head, and staggered out into the middle of a marching band. I ducked under a trombone and started running up the aisle down the middle of their formation. Passing through the brass section, I ran forward once more. My target shouldered his massive form through the musicians causing a disruption. I ducked down and ran faster, praying there weren't any cops along this leg of the parade. Explaining this would be impossible.

Musclehead pushed his way among the baton twirlers. The poor girls did their best to ignore him as his eyes roved back and forth. When he saw the young girl with the red hair braided tight against her head, Musclehead lunged for her. Somehow the Sons of Aleph must have tracked the sale of the last diamond to her. I was right behind them and trying to do one of the hardest things I could imagine: redirecting my gift. I was in the grip of the finding now. The geas was upon me. The goal was right in front of me just a few more steps. But I had to find something else. I needed to find a way to stop the Musclehead from harming an innocent girl. My talent was absolutely certain she had the last diamond and it felt like a peal of joy when he tore at her costume top and the necklace bear-ing the diamond flew free into the air. But I pushed, bearing my will down, demanding that my talent find what *I* wanted. Finding that diamond was easy, it was a given now that I'd seen it. No, I wanted a challenge. I wanted something really difficult. In that moment the twirlers launched their batons into the air and I saw my chance.

"Sorry," was all I had time to say, as I reached up above the poor little twirler to my right and caught her baton out of the air. I swung it around in a wide arc and cracked Musclehead across the back of his skull just as he was pulling the final diamond from the necklace. He slumped and struck the ground. I smacked him with the baton a few more times just for good measure. After I'd done

my best to bend it back into true, I handed the baton back to the shocked twirler with a sheepish grin. Then I plucked the last diamond from between his fingers before scrabbling for those already in Musclehead's pockets.

As soon as all of the stones were clutched in my hand, I briefly felt guilty. I was taking the girl's diamond, but you didn't leave a knife with a child. The necklace went back into Musclehead's pocket, let him explain. I turned around to discover Ione charging through the band at me, waving her gun over her head.

Usually, at the end of a search I like to enjoy the warm, golden glow of a job well done. It didn't look like I was going to get the chance this time. Just ahead of me was the color guard, a pair of band members with flags and another two holding the ends of a long banner draped over a bar that spread across the front of the band. Turning, I ran forward to leap over the banner just ahead of the baton twirlers. I crouched down and waited for Ione. As soon as she came up to the banner, I slammed the bar upward and into her jaw. Her gun went flying and she went down. I turned and ran toward the float ahead of me. I looked back only when I'd clambered up onto the flatbed. As my legs dangled over the edge, I saw Ione struggle to her feet. The Save C.J. banner lay over her and his jocular features briefly covered her face before falling off. Then the float I was on took a turn and Ione vanished from sight.

I lay back on the fake AstroTurf nailed to the truck's bed looking up at a papier-mâché float of that guy, C.J. Henderson, wrestling Cthulhu and sighed.

Bring on the warm golden glow, I thought with a satisfied smile.

As I sat up I noticed that the storm clouds overhead had finally coalesced. *This parade better end soon or we're all going to be in trouble,* I thought. Only then did I realize I felt warmth—in fact a surprising amount of it coming from my hand. The very same hand, that just happened to have all of the diamonds, which made up the heart of a djinni. The wind growled low now and there was definite circulation building in the clouds overhead. I dropped the diamonds from my burning fingers onto the Astroturf. Looking down, I discovered the setting from the earring resting on my palm.

The final diamond was free from the words binding it. What was lying on the fake grass before me was no longer a group of diamonds but rather a single teardrop-shaped gem that shone with radiant heat and crystalline facets. The Tear of El Ahzaar, soon to be followed by the rest of El Ahzaar if things kept going the way they were going. Dust lifted up from the street into the air. The Astroturf around the Tear started to smoke. From above, the snaking finger of a nascent tornado reached down from the clouds pointing toward the float and me. I begged my talent to find me a way out of this one.

Lightning crackled through clouds overhead, jumping from building to building. Everything was seconds from spiraling out of control and that's what I needed to do—control this reborn djinn. There was only one thing that might work. A flash illuminated a small child with a vitamin water in his hands—a bottle with a top on it and a large mouth. Time to bottle the djinn. I was already rolling off the float when the wind plucked the papier-mâché Cthulhu from C.J.'s grasp to go spiraling into the storm clouds overhead. A second later I had my hands on the water bottle. "I need to borrow this, to well... I need this to save the world." His little hands grasped tighter. "I swear," I said, as all of the street-lights started to glow from the ionized air. Finally, I pulled a twenty from my wallet and said, "Please just buy another one, in fact buy five."

"You're crazy, mister," was his response, but he let go of the bottle as the tip of the tornado bounced back and forth atop the buildings making the windows ripple and creak. The streets were full of people. If all of the glass blew free it would turn the street into a blender.

I ran for the float. It took three tries for me to get onto the flatbed. At that point I felt the truck accelerate and wobble under my feet. I was desperate not to fall off the back. Apparently, when the street ahead cleared, the driver decided to try to outrun the storm. Little did he know that he was pulling the source of the tempest along with him. I fell forward and began hauling myself along, one handful of Astroturf at a time. The sculpture of C.J.

began to list toward me until it blocked the view of the storm. I felt the heat of the heart of the djinni ahead of me and the burning plastic grass continued to let off a choking black smoke. The real problem now was getting the top off of the bottle in my right hand. My left firmly gripped the edge of the disintegrating Astroturf and provided my only steady anchor. The winds screamed over me and the faux C.J. loomed ever closer. In a last desperate measure, I stuck the top of the bottle between my teeth twisting until it came off in my mouth. I pulled myself up as much as possible and scooped the burning diamond teardrop into the water bottle. Letting go, my left hand pulled the top from my lips and shoved it down on top of the container sealing the heart of the djinni within. I rolled off the back of the truck and hit the pavement, the bottle cradled in my arms. A second later the papier-mâché C.J. Henderson slammed nose down onto the truck right where I'd been.

The truck drove off, the nascent tornado above fraying apart into dust devils and wisps of cloud. I sat down on the curb and laughed. In fact I had a good long laugh, because most of the people were smart enough to get off the street and the city wasn't torn apart by the resurrection of a creature of pure fire and wind. When I pulled out my phone and my tablet I was stunned to discover neither were broken. When I called Spindle he must have thought I was hysterical since I was having trouble stringing thoughts together. I started laughing once again when I discovered that the bot that was supposed to send me the information about Musclehead failed. The police still couldn't figure out exactly where the information came from but it allowed them to arrest Prester's killer when he was found in the middle of the parade. Ione had not done much better being discovered only several yards away, gun in hand terrorizing the marching band members.

I took a brief inventory. Considering the scrapes, bruises, and small cuts, I was actually in pretty good shape. The vitamin water bottle on the floor was another story though. That loose end needed tying up. I needed a place where no one would ever find the heart of the djinni again. My talent spun around and around until a mental image formed of the globe. I started my tablet up and began typing, chuckling once again. How much could a ticket for a cruise over the Marianas Trench really cost anyway?

To C.J. nothing—most especially himself—was more important than his family. This story captures that perfectly.

The Editors

Shadows of the Infinite is another of my late-night, can't-sleep, mobile-phone written stories. At the time, CJ's prognosis still had the word "hopeful" in it, so I wanted to create a story in which he won. Given that end goal, the frequent description of cancer as a battle, and CJ's love for Cthuluesque horror, the story almost wrote itself from there. And then I slept.

Leona Wisoker

Shadow of the Infinite

Leona Wisoker

THIS IS HOW I REMEMBER IT HAPPENING. I DON'T trust much these days, certainly not my fragmenting memory, but I took notes. Really good notes. He knew that I was crazy-serious about documenting things. It's one of the reasons we got along so well, one of the reasons that he called me in to help.

He was sick. I knew that going in. I'd seen cancer hit folks before, and it's never pretty. C.J. made it look worse than usual, but he'd been no prize to start with.

Oh, I'm not allowed to say that? Why, because I have tits? Five years ago, you would have laughed it off as guy talk. Fuck you. I haven't changed that much. Or maybe I've changed back. It's hard to tell, some days.

Anyway, I knew what to expect. He was down a hundred pounds at least, which hurt to see all on itself. That big goofy grin had become a pale wrinkle in a sagging face, and the beard stubble was a brisk shadow of his former mane.

Yeah, so I don't use words the way you've been taught. Lighten up, and listen. It isn't easy for me to tell this story, even with all those notes. I wasn't ever all that good at proper structure, and it's not high on my priorities just in this second.

I didn't bother telling C.J. that he looked like shit. He already knew. And I didn't tear up over him looking so sorry, either, but only because it would have confused him to no end. He has enough trouble dealing with me on a good day. Never knew me before the transition, and he's been good about it overall, but I can tell.

Never mind that. I'm trying to talk about that day he called me in to the hospital, calling in that favor I owed him from…well, never mind that either. Like I said, memory is a funny thing these days, and that's one story I'd have to get a hundred and ten percent right for it to make sense to you.

Rambling. Shouldn't ramble. Where was I? Hospital. C.J.. Right.

"I'm dying," says he, and "yeah," says me, because what else are you gonna say to that? And I'm thinking, dude, if you called me in here to pull the plug when nobody's looking, fuck you, I do not owe you that big a favor.

I'd have to look his wife in the eye afterward, you know? No way. Might as well kill myself along with him and—

Rambling. Damnit.

He didn't ask me that. He asked me something that sounded easier, if crazier, and wound up being—

Judge for yourself.

"Reggie," he says, like always—one of the little tells he has, using that name instead of Regina; okay, so I didn't exactly become Brooke Shields, whatever, it doesn't turn out the same for every-one—"you know I'm a writer. You know I write weird shit. You've read some of it, unless you've lied about that." He laughed a little, then, and I grinned back.

"Nope, no lies there," I said. "Even liked a couple of them."

That got another grin out of him. Then he said the first weird thing. "I'm beginning to think it's real. Some of it, anyway."

I just looked at him, thinking about that. "That was my previous life, C.J.," I finally said. "I don't do that stuff anymore." Because with an opening line like that, knowing what he did about me, what the hell else could he be wanting but a connection with his departed loved ones?

"No," he said, like that reaction surprised him. "Oh, I see… No. That's not it at all. I don't want a bloody séance. That's all garbage and we both know it."

I bristled a little. "I wouldn't say all. And you just admitted you believe now. At least in part."

"Not in séances," he said with regal contempt. "In the other stuff. The other realms. Demons. You know..." He lowered his voice. "Cthulhu."

I blinked a few times, trying to stay neutral, but my gaze went to the drip bag of medicines by the bed. The cord wrapped around and around, like a snake strangling the pole; I'd never seen one that didn't hang straight before, but this was clearly deliberate, so there had to be a reason. I didn't exactly *trust* doctors, but I knew there was a whole lot I didn't know about medicine. So I didn't say anything about it. Or about how weird the shadow of the IV pole looked — there was something that caught me as not quite right about it. But I put that down to hospital lighting. It has always screwed with my vision.

"Uhm," I says. "That's, uhm, interesting."

He swatted a hand at the bag, nowhere close to hitting it. "It's not the damn medication," he snapped. "I'm a writer. Been one for years. Don't you think I know the difference between hallucination and reality by now?"

There was absolutely no nice answer to that which would not burn my mouth on the way out, so I just stayed quiet.

"I've been having visions," he said, and I managed to keep my gaze on the pillow by his left ear this time instead of looking at the drip bag again. "I'm hearing things, Reggie. Stuff that's true. I hear my wife talking on the phone to her sister — while she's ten miles away at our house! And she comes in and tells me all about the conversation, and I've already heard it, word for fucking word, Reggie!"

His face had more color in it than when I'd come in, and his blood pressure count was going up. "Easy," I said. "I don't want you stroking out on me here, C.J.."

He listened to me, amazingly enough, and calmed down before he went on. "When I have these visions, it's like there's something there, something in the background, listening in. Only it's worse than that. I think it's the reason I can hear and see these things. I hear it laughing sometimes, and God, Reggie, it scares me."

I stole a look at the drip bag and didn't say anything. Because what am I gonna say that wouldn't be an outright lie?

"I haven't told anyone else," he said. "The few who would believe me would be useless, and the others would dope me up with anti-hallucinogenics."

"I don't know where you put me on that scale," I said.

"Intelligently skeptical, and analytical, but open to seeing and accepting provable facts," he said, "which is what I need."

"To do what, exactly?"

"I don't want this creature eavesdropping on my wife," C.J. says.

At this point, I'll admit I'm going straight by my notes, because I got no memory of the remaining parts of this conversation.

C.J. asked me to find a way to stop the demon, or whatever it was, from intruding into his final days like this. His wife deserved better, he said. She deserved private conversations with her family and friends, and he sure as hell didn't want to overhear her crying and cursing him anymore.

He deserved some quiet, too, he said. Which seemed fairly reasonable to me.

I had no damn idea, by my notes, if he was loony or sane. I even got permission to talk to his doctors — carefully, of course — but they didn't give me any read like he'd been acting loopy.

I wish they had. I could have walked away. But C.J., you know, for all his blustery crazy shit, he had a certain charm even then, even sick as a mangy dog, even when he wasn't trying to use that grin to get anything. And, well, by my notes, I had been feeling a little nostalgic, and wishing I hadn't left *everything* behind when I transitioned... So I said I'd look into it.

Those of you who read C.J.'s work can take a wild guess at what I found and how I found it. It's as good as mine, at any rate. My notes on everything that happened after I left his room are gone — destroyed, stolen, lost, who knows.

My memory picks up again with a four-foot-tall piece of true ugly, festering purple and blue and black, tentacles and eyes all around, and a mouth with lots of teeth located on the top of its slimy head. It stood in front of me and laughed. The sound made me want to vomit, choke on it, turn inside out and crawl away screaming, but I couldn't move.

Everything around us layered in weird shades of orange and purple and sienna. Shadows were white and red, and inverted from the shapes they should have been. Other things moved, not far away, but I couldn't see them clearly — they blended into the color distortions of the landscape. All I could see was the occasional strobe-like, shadowy flicker of colors sliding through one another.

I didn't want to see the things casting those shadows, not if they were anything like the one in front of me. It looked like a demon had fucked a Dalek and forced a hybrid cross with an anemone in the womb.

The air smelled of thousand-year-old Dorito farts and worn-out shoes that a hellcat had pissed into. And past that image, trust me, you do *not* want to hear any more scenic details of that place. Or if you do, go find it for yourself. I don't want to remember it for you.

"He wants us to stop eavesdropping on him?" the demon-horror said when it was done laughing for the moment. "And what of the years he spent eavesdropping on *us*? Encouraging his fellow horror writers to eavesdrop on our lives, never asking permission? And distorting the tales into vile slanders. Giving us weaknesses we do not possess! Ignoring our greatest strengths! No, human; you mortal, pathetic creature. He has earned his disquiet. We will make him suffer."

"I thought his stories painted you as pretty strong," I said. "And you can't blame him entirely. He was just following the path of those before him, back to Frankenstein's Monster and beyond. Go scream at folks like Lovecraft. Why pick on C.J.?"

"That is our business," it said as haughtily as anything that ugly can manage. "And he is not the first or only to feel our wrath in his last days."

I watch eyes. It's a habit from a long life of picking out the best line to feed a client about their dearly departed. And even with this many eyes, some of them have to move together to focus properly. So I caught the glance, and I looked.

One of the tentacles winding out from the demon's body looked strange. More translucent than colored. More....plastic. And spiral, not straight, as though it were wrapping around an invisible pole. It gleamed, from time to time, as though artificial light sporadically traced along the curves.

Like that hospital IV drip. The damn ugly creature had somehow diverted it. C.J. wasn't getting medicine; he was getting demon poison. Or maybe it was sucking the life out of him with the connection. I don't know, to this day. Again, no notes left, jewelry hazy in spots. Memory. Memory hazy.

Memory is tricky. I think I lunged at the drip line once or twice. I think the creature laughed again, freezing me in place. I think I did vomit and start to choke on it this time.

"Some reward for real immortality." I clearly remember saying that at some point. The creature stopped tormenting me and stared, every eye that could turn my way focused on my face.

"We *are* immortal, stupid human," it said.

"No, you're not," I told it. "You can be hurt, even killed. I can tell, because you breathe. Your heart beats. You show clear emotions and thoughts, and I'll bet gold that you even have loved ones. Those are the strengths you think C.J. and his fellow writers missed or distorted."

Which was a total wild guess, but seriously, if you've ever read Lovecraft horror stories, what the hell else could this thing be whining about in terms of being "misundastood"?

"But you're wrong," I went on when the thing just stared at me without answering. "What C.J. did, and his fellow writers did, was to evoke the exact things you see as your strengths within their readers. People who read these stories learn about life, and faith, and loss, and to face what frightens us, and how to overcome it. And how to laugh through the pain. Aren't those all things you value? Isn't that more of an honor than an insult?"

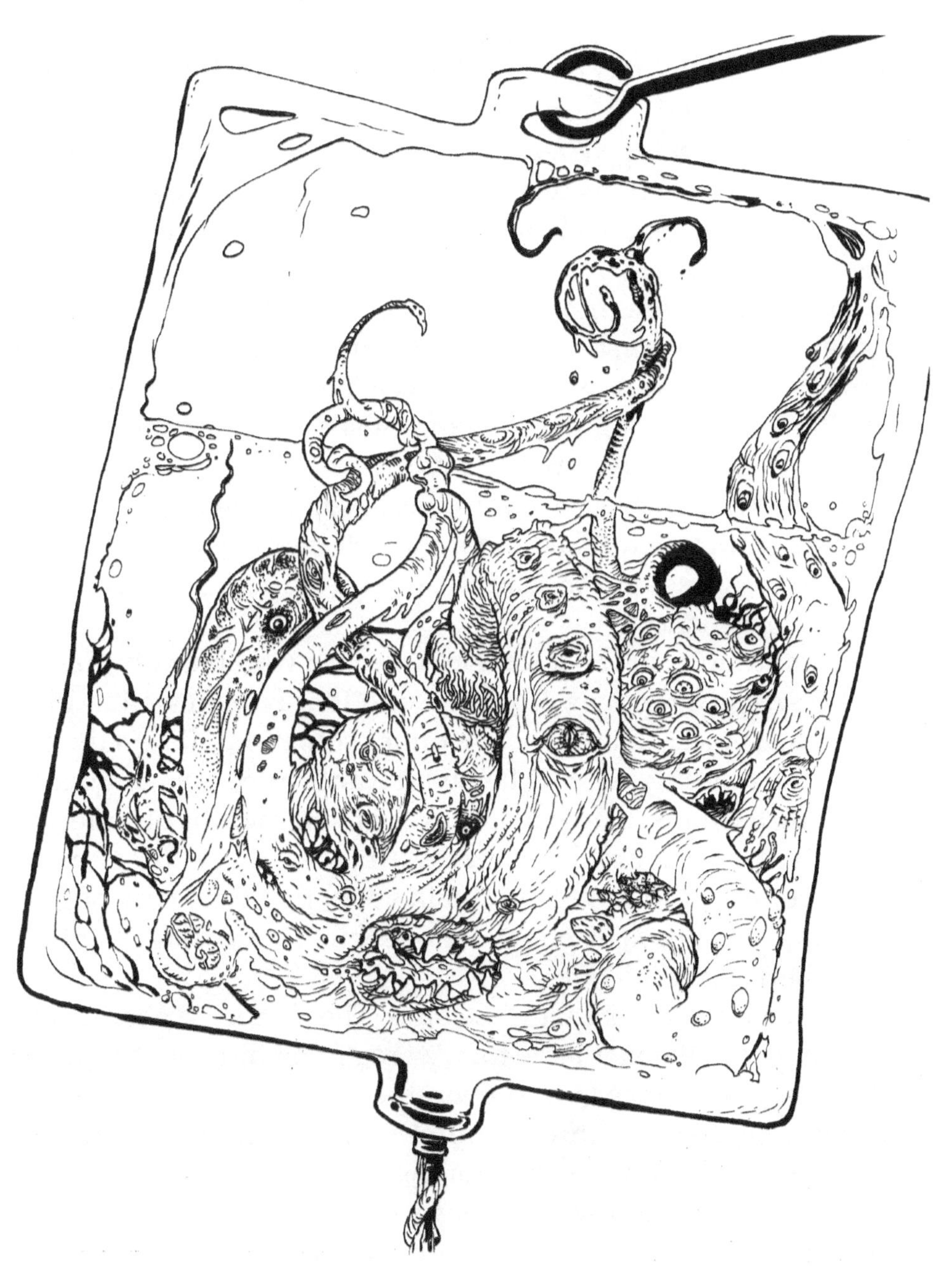

It babbled to itself, as if arguing with invisible friends. Given how that was, actually, a possibility, and that those invisible friends were not at *all* likely to buy my impromptu bullshit argument, I took advantage of the distraction to go for the cord again. This time I grabbed it. And yanked, as hard as I could. It was like pulling my own guts out through my teeth, and if that makes no sense in print, let me tell you, it made a hell of a lot less sense in action. But *that* memory is totally clear.

Next thing I remember is lying on the floor next to C.J.'s hospital bed. He was sleeping and the machines were all beeping and the IV stand was nowhere to be seen. Nurses and doctors came flying in like an avenging army, and hustled me out and into the arms of a very unamused police officer.

And now I'm in a psych ward, because I made the mistake of telling the truth when asked what the hell happened. Look, I was rattled. And hysterical. And shortly after that, heavily doped up. I never stood a chance.

C.J. comes to visit me a lot. He's the one who brought me my notebooks. Snuck them in, of course, and I keep them well hidden. And he has copies, just in case. I wonder sometimes if he's the one that has the missing pages. Maybe he wants to be able to go after that demon for himself, to pay it back for those months of suffering.

I don't ask. I don't really want those pages back. I don't want to remember how I did it. We don't talk about that time very often — the doctors are always listening, for one thing, and I don't want C.J. stuck in here alongside me.

He's looking much better these days. The doctors say something was wrong with the medicine they were giving him, but they can't explain how the cancer — and even the blood clots they were so worried about — went into complete remission overnight. The cancer has stayed gone for six months now.

C.J. is, of course, the only person who believes me. That's okay. He's solemnly promised to never write another word of Cthulusque horror. I hear he's actually going into Regency romances these days, which might just be worse. I might be misremembering that too. Did he actually say Regency? Or did he say *rodeo romances*? It might even have involved something that sparkled. Maybe he does belong in here with me after all.

No, he's a writer. He knows how to handle the outside world. He'll manage.

I'd rather stay here, to be honest. I don't want to leave just yet. It's quiet, compared to *that place;* the screams and yells of my fellow residents are almost musical, even at their worst. And I don't have to pretend I'm all right. I can scream and gibber with all the rest, and nobody minds a bit. That's awfully nice some days.

It's the laughter. I still hear it the background, you see. It makes me turn all inside out and choke on my brain...and the shadows haven't ever quite looked *right* since I came back.

I think they've started eavesdropping on *me* now....

Though he wrote in many genres and styles, Mythos is where C.J. shone. He would have loved this story, which combines both Lovecraft and a so-bad-it's-great B-movie.

The Editors

C.J. Henderson made me a character in his stories. I am the real Professor Goward. Thus it seems natural for me to write a first-person narrative as an old professor at Miskatonic University. It will take no great detective skills on your part to discern the two fictional sources for my tale. It is made up of equal parts of H.P. Lovecraft's "The Mound" and that classic of Mexican cinema, *The Robot versus the Aztec Mummy.*

Robert M. Price

Digging Up Doomsday

Robert M. Price

Let me hasten to assure you, any serious colleagues who may be reading this, that I resisted the whole idea. The proposal reeked from the first of the Public Relations department rather than any serious academic interest. I still prefer to think the whole thing was a bid to attract the History Channel or the Discovery Channel and draw some much-needed attention to Miskatonic and to polish up some of its long vanished fame. The danger was that it would serve instead to revive its even older infamy. The school had long been haunted (if I may use the word) by the foulest of rumors, sometimes abetted, I will admit, by the absurd stunts of some of our more venturesome students, mainly majors in the fields of decadent poetry and medieval metaphysics. Most of these scandals, occasions for the momentary relief of public ennui, and at a high price for the school's reputation, had evaporated years before, thanks to the short attention span of the public. And here it all came again, or threatened to. What proposal portended such mischief? I see that, in my professorial way, I have forgotten to tell you.

As I imagine you know, there has been considerable speculation (to put it very mildly) on the terminal date scheduled for the human race on the ancient and enigmatic "Mayan calendar." Transnumerated into our dates, that Central American disk concludes abruptly with the year 2012. Why does it do that? The more hysterically inclined like to think that the old Mayan savants were in possession of some cosmic secret that there would thenceforth be no history to bother to schedule! It reminded me of some scamp's penciled notation on a church office calendar I once saw: "October 10: Second Coming of Christ. October 11: Deacons meeting." Not likely. Only in the case of the Mayans, they realized there could be no deacons meetings to schedule after 2012. And someone at Miskatonic floated the idea that a couple of the school's archaeology and anthropology faculty ought to make a trip to Mexico and Central America (I don't believe he or she even knew where the Mayans were located!) to fathom the secret. You already know what I thought the real motivation was: crass condescension to the tastes of the mob. But at the same time I thought to myself: if it turns out the Mayans had some inside knowledge, why, at least there would soon be an end to the dreadful faculty meetings at Miskatonic.

I was asked to head up the "expedition." Now Miskatonic University was once known for having mounted genuine expeditions worthy of the name, though the results were never widely credited (when they were publicly circulated). This, I felt sure, would not be one of them. More in the nature of a summer school student dig, an exercise in using the tools of the trade. Now I am a New Englander from way back. I was not even a specialist in the archaeology of the Central American region (though neither was anyone else in the department), but I was encouraged to learn that I would have the company of Hector Eccheveria, a brilliant Mexican American scholar and anthropologist. To be frank, I wondered if my participation in the venture was not rendered superfluous once they had drafted Eccheveria, but he pled his superficial acquaintance with archaeology and thus deprived me of my best bet for escaping the silly project. So we planned our trip and assembled our equipment.

Among these accoutrements, I was nonplussed at the sight of a set of heavy boxes, heavily braced and amply cushioned, implying solid but delicate machinery of some type. I asked Eccheveria what might be in this imposing luggage. He told me, with inflections of shared mystery, that it was a "gift" from the engineering department: a kind of automaton to gather specimens from hostile or toxic terrain where human beings, with our vulnerabilities, might fear to tread. It was, he ventured, basically the same sort of thing as the "rover" that had trodden its patient way across the sands of Mars, sending back data to scientists who wished they could have been on the scene in person. We would of course be on the scene, a more mundane one I hoped, but the contraption might come in handy. I said I hoped it would justify the cost of extra sets of hands to lug the boxes through the jungle, or into the mountains, or wherever we might end up. But, all told, I much preferred the prospect of Tsetse flies making kamikaze runs on the robot's metal shell than on my poor flesh.

I will not try your patience with the dreary business of trip preparations and customs permissions, especially for unorthodox equipment whose purpose even we could not readily explain, it being in the nature of an insurance policy should we encounter hypothetical perils. But we arrived in rural Mexico, seeking out scattered enclaves of isolated Mayan tribes (of which some 28 linger still). Why go so far, one might ask, when our own American cities harbor such a wealth of hardy Mexican specimens? All I need say is that the growing Mexican population was, if not a dry well, then a well blocked up. Those residing in the United States as naturalized citizens wanted to look forward to their new lives as Americans, not back to the misty ways of their primitive ancestors. They tended to be ashamed of their roots (unfortunately, as I view it) and to want nothing so much as to forget them. On the other hand, those Mexicans who entered the country illegally resisted the interrogation of people like myself and Eccheveria, since such information as we sought seemed to them to constitute evidence of an unwelcome alien presence. Thus we had to leapfrog our own hard-working Mexican population, rich sources of popular oral tradition as they might have been, and go a step closer to the source, south of the border.

You might expect to read that Eccheveria and I made a beeline for the famous ruins of Chichen-Itza, but we did not. Pretty near every square foot of that spectacular site had been thoroughly mapped, photographed, and analyzed already, and we had availed ourselves of those (for our purposes) paltry results. So we sought less obvious sources of information and tradition. In Guatemala, we began with extensive interviews with recently urbanized Mayans, simply because they were closer to our transportation hub. These generous individuals, while flattered at the interest we showed in their indigenous culture, were, if anything, too eager to please us. At first we imagined we had hit the jackpot, as ostensible family traditions about the Mayans and their calendar keeping abounded. The calendar, some said, was the product of the astronomical wisdom, or "starry wisdom," of the ancient Mayans, the "old ones." Did these savants mean to set a limit to human life on the earth? Many said yes, though they seemed little troubled by the increasingly imminent prospect. It soon became clear that most of this intriguing lore had been derived from American and European tabloid television. They were merely feeding back to us the same junk food they had imported from us to begin with.

Next we sought guides into the far reaches, to enclaves of unspoiled Native Mayan Indians. Here even Eccheveria's fluent Spanish proved largely useless, and we both had to rely upon his sketchier knowledge of Central American tribal dialects. (I had a rudimentary knowledge of the languages of the Micmac Indian and other New England peoples, but this proved absolutely futile.) It was by no means easy to be sure we were asking the right questions, or being understood. But, comparing our notes by lamp light in our tightly screened tent, my comrade and I began to think we were hearing again and again about the same group of priests or kings, called the *Ku'hul Ajau* ("holy lords"), apparently now extinct, who had once transmitted the inherited secret traditions of the calendar and its meaning. We were much inclined to trust this evidence because of the fact that the calendar was known to these villagers and tribesmen when it was no longer of any worldly use to them.

On we pressed, back into Mexico as we spent more and more of the merciless summer with little to show for it. We followed the same procedure as before, spreading out from the cities to the countryside. Again, most of the lore we received turned out to be imported New Age drivel the origin of which the television-watching peasants seemed to have forgotten. How difficult, no matter where the anthropologist sets his intrepid foot, to discover native souls uncorrupted by Western popular culture. Not to romanticize primitivism! But where it exists, as the old ethnologists knew well, it may serve as a living fossil against which to measure one's theories of human cultural development in the past. But, in the wake of colonial, commercial, and missionary expansion, such flowers are rare indeed. I will only remark how tired I became of hearing Mayan Indians tell me they were descendants of the Lamanites of the Book of Mormon! Others had been there before us!

Through most of our expedition I cursed the attendant bulk of our boxed robotic equipment. But one day I repented and became quite glad we had brought it along. Persistent hints, including a few dire warnings, had beckoned Eccheveria and me on what we swore would be our last wild goose chase. There was an almost inaccessible wilderness region from which few had ever returned without a distinctly contagious malady which some connected with the wholesale disappearance of over ninety per cent of the Mayan population back in 950 AD. The legend had it that this very place was the carefully guarded retreat of the *Ku'hul Ajau*, and that the priest-kings had long ago defied lesser mortals to trespass on their preserve. The Mayan culture, like the better known Aztecs, was known for practicing human sacrifice, but the victims were supposedly recruited from rival tribes. The oral reports we now heard suggested that this was not quite the case. Rather, it seemed that this priestly caste supplied the sacrificial victims from their own ranks. Once a priest reached a certain age, having fathered offspring to carry on for him, he happily yielded to a sacrifice in which his colleagues participated with pious gustatory glee. It was a corpse-eating cult not unlike that which Madame Alexandra David-Neel had once claimed throve in mystical Tibet. I had always been inclined to dismiss her chilling travelogue tales as Blavatsky-style fictions, but that such a degraded ritual should survive in remote outposts of the world should not strike the field researcher as especially improbable. Eccheveria and I decided that we had to follow up these rumors.

We had driven as close to our destination as we dared, for fear of destroying our tires. We saw close by a low mesa not recorded on any map, quite an anomaly in this day and age, when computers can pinpoint any desired location by means of spy satellites. Through our field glasses we could just make out atop the table rock what appeared to be a circle of stone stumps, suggesting a much eroded and therefore very ancient structure like Stonehenge, hence an astronomical calendar of sorts. I admit, this was the very first time during our whole trip that I had begun to feel any sense of hope, and of relief from the constant feeling of embarrassment that we were wasting our time royally. If there were any lead to follow to success, this had to be it. Eccheveria and I were eager to ascend the butte, but there were subtle signs recommending caution. For one thing, the crowned plateau appeared to occupy the center of a markedly arid zone where no scrub grass grew. There was no sound of animal or of nature. We thought at once of the rumored plague, and of the decimated population long gone. Neither of us harbored any thought of leaving the place unexamined, but we did agree the time had arrived to assemble the research drone. Unboxing the heavy, chromed pieces of the mechanism, my comrade and I sat in the midst of the great boxes and cylinders like flabbergasted parents trying to assemble a child's bicycle on Christmas Eve.

We had made significant progress when Eccheveria looked up from our slow labor and cried out, "Look! Someone's coming! At the base!" As he rose to investigate, I strained to look, managing to see only a stunted, slow-moving human figure. I am dreadfully near-sighted under the best circumstances, and here I had the heat haze to deal with, too. The field glasses sharpened my focus, however, and I saw, at a safe distance, what Eccheveria must be seeing close up at nearly the same moment, for I heard him scream. I forgot everything else around me, including that I possessed a set of hands holding binoculars, which fell unheeded to the ground.

All I could see at the center of my tunnel vision was, well, what *looked* like a gray-skinned man marked with tattoos and livid scars, – *with no head.* Sightless as he must be, he nonetheless trod a straight path for Eccheveria, who stood stock still with fright, making himself an easy target for the shuffling hulk he otherwise should easily have evaded. I regained my self-possession sufficiently to yell out to him to run. He did not, and in a moment his corpse toppled over like a felled tree. The creature, all massive shoulders and biceps, had decapitated Eccheveria, as if inducting him into some unholy fellowship. And now he was turning in my direction.

The drone was complete. I was pretty sure I knew how to direct it. I saw what its camera eyes picked up on my view screen, but the robot had been designed for use at considerable distances, albeit where previous aerial scrutiny would have foreseen a clear path. But I stood at no great distance from the headless golem which now made its ineluctable way toward me. I could see it quite plainly. A moment before, I had taken for granted that the trudging thing was another automaton, much like our own, posted as a guard by some other explorer jealous of his privacy. But now I saw that it had the appearance of an organic being. It might have been a metal skeleton zipped up in a plastic or rubber container to feign human flesh, but what would have been the point?

All this floated absently through my mind as I sought frantically to master the controls of the drone. The headless thing, whose skin I saw was mottled and wrinkled, suggesting an antique fragility belying its obvious strength, came on and on. At once I grasped the requisite sequence of switches and buttons, and our hitherto dormant expedition partner came to clanking life. It possessed three great arms, at more or less human shoulder level, for it had been designed to heft sizeable boulders blocking its way at desired targets. I now put that steely strength to a different use, as I sent the robot into battle against its rival titan. I could but imagine what my unconscious (?) opponent saw as he embarked on his death match with my own mechanical champion, but, judging from the television monitor on the "face" of the robot, my own peering visage must have been projected there, by a tiny camera such as one finds in desk computers. A grotesque picture indeed! One combatant a headless Mayan mummy, the other a lumbering mechanical man with an old professor's face!

The mummified guardian, however animated (and in the press of events, I simply set that impossible question aside), had evidently seen its better days. Intended, so I would imagine, as some sort of horrific scarecrow, it no longer possessed the power to defend itself. My robotic arms easily plucked one of his fleshly limbs off, kicked its footing out from under it, and trampled it into dusty ruin. Grateful that the combat had carried the two figures away from me, I was relieved not to be breathing in the foul gases and dust billowing up from the mummy's remains. Finding a button to activate a fan, I blew most of the miasma away so I might scrutinize what was left. Some trinkets had adorned the walking corpse. There appeared nothing extraordinary about them.

But then, as I was about to recall the robot and go take a closer look at the form of my fallen friend, I noticed something after all. The trunk of the mummy had fallen on a foot-long cylinder that must have been somehow pinned to its leathery flesh. I picked it up with the blunt pincer of the drone and retrieved it. Setting it aside for the nonce, I made ready to apply the mechanism to yet another use alien to its planned function: digging a trench deep enough to contain the remains of Hector Eccheveria so that neither tomb robbers nor carrion beasts might get to it. The mighty thews of the robot were easily equal to the task.

I considered waiting to open the tube of peculiar blue-green metal back at my cheap hotel room, but I somehow felt it was part of my unfinished business at this strange site, so I pitched a tent near the rented truck and built a fire. By its blaze I gave the metal container a closer look, hoping to find an unspoiled release mechanism. To my great surprise and relief, I had the thing open in minutes. It had resisted corrosion marvelously well. At first I had taken the odd hue of the thing for a coat of tarnish, but now I could see it represented the normal color of the unidentifiable metal. One intrigue led to another as I unscrewed the tube to discover, as I had dearly hoped, a rolled up manuscript within it.

There was no danger of the air or of my touch causing the manuscript to crumble, as it, too, seemed to be made of a strange metal, thin almost as aluminum foil yet durable. It had been inscribed in some manner, though I did not think it was ink any more than the scroll itself was papyrus or parchment. Envisioned barriers were falling like dominoes as I saw by my firelight that the text was written in Proto-Mayan, the well known antecedent to the numerous surviving modern local tongues spoken by Mayan tribes in Central and South America. I had only a rough acquaintance with the language but had brushed up on it in preparation for this trip. I was now doubly glad I had done so.

Glyphs common to the written text and to the tattooed hide of the dead, headless form implied the identity of the writer with the lifeless carcass I had sent the robot to destroy. The author proclaimed himself as the last of the *Ku'hul Ajau*, the possessor and guardian of a history that must be preserved, even beyond death, so that the old ones might come again and restore the life of the earth. I will transcribe here a portion of my rough translation.

It was the wrath of the old ones, neglected for too long in worship, that brought famine upon the land with its blaze that burns the stomachs of children. But those ones did not forsake us wholly. Many of the people had died, and such was the weakness of the rest that we could no longer give them burial. But in our direst hour the Man came from below the land, saying he had come from another kingdom to help us. If only we would gather our remaining strength and come with him. He looked strange, so we feared a long journey to a land unknown and far away. But he said the journey would be as short as his had been, and he had left his home but a day earlier. Great was the number who followed him. Many murmured as he led us first to the mountains we had always known. We were too hungry and frail to make the ascent. But here he showed us a cave and a path we had never seen before, leading down and ever downward, some feared, to the land of the unrighteous dead. But only death waited above, so we went down. Past great pillars of dripping stone we went, now and again catching up the wriggling eyeless cave fish to ease our hunger.

Our great fears were renewed when we neared the gate of the under-earth kingdom, for it was guarded by the shuffling dead! Surely we had after all entered the hell of our fathers. Their heads were gone, no doubt the prey of vultures. But the Man laughed at our fears and welcomed us to a kingdom of life and joy where all, even the dead, had their role to play for the good of all. There was plenty of food and enough room for us, though we were very many. But we were to pay a severe price. We became the slaves of the cave people. They took our women from us as they chose and they took for themselves the best of our produce from the strange mushroom farms below and the herds of pale creatures we tended. Most of us had been free farmers up above. We had been poor, but the land afforded us liberty. No more. Not below.

Worst of all, our masters sought to take from us the true religion of the old ones. Every oppression we could stand, but not this one. This we could not allow. My people came to me, singly and in groups large and small, and all begged me to strike a blow for freedom, to avenge the people and to vindicate their gods, lest in return the gods smite us even worse for our faithlessness. I told them how the day of vengeance was already set, and that no man might hasten it. Inscribed on our calendars had been the date of Judgment Day, the solstice of eleven hundred years hence. On that day the sun should rise in the midst of the [Milky Way] band of stars in the heavens. And then the stars should be right for the old ones to return, for even they must obey the laws written in the heavens. All knew this, but it provided little comfort.

At length no one came to me anymore, since I had no comfort to give. I sank into sad despair for the sake of my people. And finally I knew there was something I could do, perilous blasphemy though it be. There was indeed nothing I or any man might do to hasten the end, when the old world should die and a new one, without the passing of time or death, should dawn. But there was a way to unleash the terrible wrath of the old ones before the fullness of time. Only death should follow, drawing no distinction between righteous and wicked, between believers and infidels, but at least the oppressed should enjoy the sleep of oblivion for his respite. At least the whip should no more harvest his thinning blood. His enemies should no longer rape his daughters.

But then, I knew, I myself should be carried away in the same flood. And in that case, none should be left when the stars came right. None should know the proper words and dances with which to revive the old ones. I was the last of the holy lords of K'hul-lu. There was no one to whom I might tell the words and the dances, to perform the rite centuries hence. But the Great K'hul-lu appeared to me in a dream and told me what to do. He had heard the bitter groans of his people, and he would sweep away their sufferings, together with the wickedness of the cave kingdom. They, too, had once been his people, but they no longer truly believed. They were ripe for judgment, and judgment should fall like an ax. It remained for me to chant the execration spell and to release the power of the old ones as they lay dreaming. For even in sleep they did not lack power, though it was left to their servants to draw upon it. That I determined to do.

There remained the puzzle of bequeathing to the future the knowledge required to set loose the old ones from their slumberous caverns at the appointed date. But my lord revealed that to me as well. I shall write down here the words and the steps to recall the old ones when the stars come right. They are simple enough. And then I shall go to those who animate the mummies of the dead to serve as guardians of the gates of this underground kingdom, and I shall pay them handsomely to make me one of their deathless, lifeless slaves. They shall conceal about my person the very scroll I now inscribe, and when the day shall come round eleven centuries hence, a man shall come and find what I have written. In this way, the knowledge of the end of the age shall survive unto the day itself. May K'hul-lu prosper the plan and one day emerge radiant from his concealment.

I rolled the metallic leaf up and replaced it in its canister. The author had plainly expected to ignite some sort of preliminary Armageddon down there in the subterranean kingdom. He expected that none should survive. Had it happened? He had planned to employ some magical means. This I, as a man of science, could hardly credit. And yet there was the headless guardian, ostensibly the mummy of the author himself. I had seen that. I had seen the dead man walking. The headless man. I decided I must try to verify some measure of the implicit tale. I was not eager to venture into the downward shaft which the mummy must have been guarding. I had taken quite enough personal risk, and there was no sense in Eccheveria and myself both succumbing. So I decided to fire up the robot again. It should, under my direction, seek out the opening and descend as far as it could. I ought to be able to videotape whatever its infrared sensors picked up.

In the event, however, the opening of the shaft, once I found it, turned out to be blocked only a few yards down by an impenetrable wall of boulders. Nor was the shaft stable, for the attempts of the robot to displace a few of the smaller stones touched off a new rockslide, and the mechanism must have been destroyed, at least disabled, in the crushing impact.

Exhausted, I lay beside the fire as it died down, heedless of the growing cold, all the time seeking my own best council as to what to do. The trek on which I and the unfortunate Hector Eccheveria had been sent had actually attained its goal, albeit at the cost of Hector's life. The scroll contained the answers to two mysteries that had long confounded scholars: why did almost the whole Mayan population disappear eleven centuries ago? As many had surmised, the answer was famine. But not wholly that. And who would believe the rest? And why had the Mayans ended their calendar on the 2012 solstice? Had they believed the world would end? Yes, it seems they did, though they expected a strange new one to replace it. But to report these findings meant explaining and defending the absolutely impossible things I had seen in the past day. How did you say you obtained the scroll, Professor? And why did Professor Eccheveria not return with you? You will say that any lie one might concoct would sound more plausible than the strange truth. But that doesn't help if the truth is inherently unbelievable. No imaginable lie, or story, could come near covering it. And I am no good as a liar. Anything I might say would sound so suspicious as to incriminate me.

And besides, for me to publicize the revelations of this strange metal scroll would only be to try to put out the fire of hysteria with gasoline. I do not want to play into the hands of such fanatics whose chief vindicator and champion I should immediately become.

You know, I believe that I shall follow our ancient friend's example and have this written statement buried with me, though, rest assured, I will not seek to hasten the day of my death or have myself mummified! But this way, should anyone discover my text long after the fact, my report may after all be believed since no conceivable reason for a lie or a prank would remain after I am so long dead and gone. And to protect the secret, I shall return the Proto-Mayan scroll to the dust of the ages. I shall not destroy it, heavens no; as a scholar I cannot commit such a crime. But I believe I shall return to the informal grave of my esteemed colleague and commit to his chilly embrace the great discovery that is rightly his. I shall place the cylinder in the stiff hands of his headless corpse and bury the body once again. I shall tell the authorities Hector was waylaid and murdered by local brigands, one of the very dangers they warned us about.

All is back to normal. The University Chapel was the scene of a fine memorial service for Hector Eccheveria. No blame attaches to me. Painful memories plague me, but that is only natural. They will pass. Somehow I fear I shall not be so easily rid of an awful recurring dream which plagues me. In it I find myself again on the plain where I buried Hector. I get into the truck and start to drive away. But I seem to hear a disturbance behind me: the scratching and sliding of earth and stones. And, though I dare not look back, I cannot stop the mental image of Hector's headless body, clutching the metal tube, emerging from his resting place to assume the duties of his predecessor. Nothing could persuade me to return to that spot in waking life, but then I have not long to wait to find out how much of the dream, and the Mayan legend, is true.

We've already said this, but it was never truer than here. C.J. pushed boundaries. He challenged his readers to think and not assume. This is short and simple, but poignant. It is also previously unpublished. Enjoy.

The Editors

First Publications rights graciously relinquished by Villainous Press, donated for the purpose of this C.J. Henderson tribute anthology.

Sorrow

C.J. Henderson

"There is no greater sorrow than to recall a
time of happiness when in misery."
Dante

"The end of all beauty, that is sorrow."
He flew on, remembering her words; tears
such as an angel might weep dampening his
cheeks. The irony of it all stung him, drove
him onward. The kindness in her eyes when she had spoken to him
last, her gaiety. She had been striving to cheer them all, as she so
often did. His troops were a sour lot, easily distracted, often fool-
ish. But, they loved her as he did, and would die for her.

As he would.

She had ruled them with a strong hand, but they were of a type
that needed such. His kind would have responded to none other;
could have respected nothing less. But, where one who sat a
monarch's throne through strength and fear alone would have
eventually lost the loyalty of such warriors, she had not, for she
knew what they needed.

Thought of as only brutes and savages by all others, she had
taken them in, given them more than shelter, more than a home.
She had given them purpose.

Nikko tried not to think of his beloved mistress for a moment.
He needed to concentrate on the ascent, to keep his focus so that the
others might maintain theirs. As they flew higher, straight and
strong, to the clouds—through them, above them—their com-

mander clamped his teeth closed, grinding them, masking the pain in his bleeding heart.

Their queen was dead.

Taken from them by a monster from some terrible beyond, it had all ended in a moment. Their wondrous princess, destroyed in her own palace — and they had been helpless to do anything. Their mistress had commanded them to hold back, and had taken the invaders' challenge upon herself. Never one to risk the lives of others before her own, she had faced the enemy, and she had triumphed. He remembered he had been laughing, screaming with happiness at his queen's victory.

And then, somehow, in a twisted, splashing moment, it had all gone wrong. Before he or any of his fellows could comprehend what had happened, she was gone — vaporized. Disintegrated. Her great and good and kind heart taken from them —

Forever.

As the air began to thin around himself and his troops, Nikko gave the signal to his fellows that they should begin their descent. They had climbed as far as their wings could take them, clawed their way to the greatest height possible so that their return might be a thing of thundering swiftness.

Rushing toward the ground, arms at their sides, wings cutting the wind, tails straight behind them, the now-purposeless battalion darkened the sky as they rushed back toward the ground. Each and every one of them, their grieving hearts straining within their noble chests, stared forward at the rushing blur racing to meet them.

They had always said they would go where she went. That they would follow her anywhere.

That they would die for their queen.

Some might have called her wicked. The ignorant had labeled her a witch. But the Mobat legion knew better. She had been their goddess.

And, knowing they would be reunited with her soon, the winged monkeys of Oz sang out at the sight of the nearing ground waiting to embrace them.

Their sorrowful hearts filling with joy.

And if there was any parting wisdom C.J. would have wanted to leave to the world…it is this.

The Editors

The title of "Every Second of Every Day" is taken from a little bit of inspiration C.J. was fond of sharing with his fellow writers. When people complained they had no time to write or wished they could write more, C.J. gently reminded them that we all choose to do exactly what we do, every second of every day. In other words, you're in control of your time and how you use it. You can decide or you can let other people decide for you, but only you can know the best way to spend your time. And only you can make the time for writing. Personally, I think the idea expands to much more than that to include the fact that as creative people we are the only ones who can choose the path we follow. Every second of every day, when we write, we choose what we write, how we write, and who we write for. With that as a jumping off point, I wrote my story based on many of the odd and interesting experiences I had at conventions over the years, often with CJ, as well as having witnessed many times how CJ could turn someone's thinking around with even the briefest of interactions.

James Chambers

Every Second of Every Day

James Chambers

OF ALL THE TALL TALES PASSED DOWN THROUGH the decades about his great ancestor, the poet Gao Chi Lin, of all Gao's stories and poems collected in slim, yellowed volumes in a place of honor on the Lin family bookshelf, the one tale Henry Lin believed the least but loved the most told the "absolute God's truth" of how the Grand Canyon came to exist. That one, rich yarn easily claimed all credit for Henry's love of storytelling and all things imaginary. Comic, yet filled with wonder, the tale had lit a fire in a young Henry Lin that his mother had spent the last fifteen years trying to extinguish. Her efforts so far unrewarded, she yet clung to hope that her eldest son might still come to his senses, chuck away his literary aspirations, and earn a computer science degree. Or at least become a lawyer. She so regretted the day she'd read that story to her wide-eyed boy sitting on her lap that she reminded him every chance she got.

Take this morning, for instance. As Henry packed his car for the trip to AstonishingCon, his mother stood on the Lin family's front stoop, arms crossed, tapping her toe against the bricks in a disapproving rhythm.

"I never would've read you a word of your Great-Great-Great-Grand Uncle Gao's work if I'd known your life would end up like this," Henry Lin's mother said.

Shoving another box of his first novel, *The Mercurial Hearts of the Stars*, into the trunk of his twenty-year-old Saturn, Henry squinted at his mother, and said, "You mean *wind* up like this, not end."

"I mean *end.*"

"What the heck, Ma? I'm only twenty-three. My life's not over."

"Matter of opinion," she said.

"Ma, let it go. This is who I am. I'm an author, okay?"

"If you were a garbage man, I could say my son is a waste removal *engineer*, or even a community hygiene *specialist*. At least those jobs sound like *real* work. But what can I tell my friends on poker night? 'Oh, my son, he works very hard. He spends all day *authoring.*' What is that? *Authoring.* It sounds like something you do when you have pneumonia."

"I'm a writer, Ma. Tell them I write."

"I write too. I write the grocery list. I wrote the checks for your education. I guess that makes me an author, too, huh?"

With that, Henry's mother stormed inside her house and slammed the front door.

Henry sighed and slammed the trunk in reply.

Shaking his head, he climbed behind the wheel and buzzed down the road, finally en route to his first public appearance as a published author. Five boxes of his novel—hot off the presses from Loki's Library Press—sat in the trunk. At twenty-five copies a box, he only hoped he'd stocked enough. Signed copies sold fast, he'd heard, and he'd hate to sell out the first day. There were worse problems to worry about, he supposed, though none rushed to mind. Instead, he thought about the story his mother hated.

First thing that morning, he'd reread the tale of Gao and the Monkey King for inspiration.

Gao, himself—Henry's family said generation after generation—swore by the yarn's veracity. Henry knew better, of course. Not that he doubted the hard work and suffering of which his uncle wrote. Not at all. He had, in fact, once confirmed enough details to verify that old Gao had indeed labored himself to the bone and near to death under miserable circumstances helping to build the Transcontinental Railroad. Sweaty, thankless, backbreaking work done alongside thousands of other Chinese immigrants. All of them paid peanuts and fed slop to build the prime artery of a young nation. Henry's family took pride in their link to history, and for that, Henry honored his long-dead Great-Great-Great Grand Uncle.

What he admired about him, though, was the very thing he doubted, yet at the same time held closer to his heart than his mother's oh-so-conditional love: the tale Gao spun about how he prayed to the Monkey King to relieve his suffering and punish his abusive railroad bosses. Night after night Gao had proclaimed his woes until the fickle simian deity, outraged by the slop served to the Chinese workers, deigned to grant Gao's desire. To strike at the bosses, the Monkey King roused the Eternal Dragon who lived in the earth to undo the track the workers built each day; and the repeated setbacks robbed the railroad barons of their fortunes and their peace of mind. But the Monkey King, Gao's tale expounded, pushed the Eternal Dragon too far. He stoked the great beast to a rage during which he not only destroyed the railroad-in-progress but also forged the Grand Canyon overnight. A much more romantic and satisfying explanation for hundreds of miles of geological majesty than centuries of erosion caused by the Colorado River. Yet one that, Henry knew, possessed no more substance than a dream. Still the tale testified to his Great-Great-Great-Grand Uncle's powerful imagination and storytelling mastery. And by the end of his first day at AstonishingCon, Henry found himself wishing it were all true because much like old Gao, he desperately wanted the Monkey King to save him and deal righteous mischief to his evil abusers.

The list of injustices inflicted upon Henry began only ten miles from home.

First, the traffic. A horrible, torturous, bumper-to-bumper quilt of vehicles trapped at a crawl for seemingly infinite minutes, only to break suddenly—for no apparent reason—into an easy fifty-mile-an-hour glide for three minutes max before reverting to a metal-and-plastic death march. Hours later, by the time Henry traveled far enough down the New Jersey Turnpike to see overhead traffic signs flashing "Major Delays" — of which he was already damn well aware — the first microscopic cracks had already spread through his sanity.

They only deepened when he exited the Turnpike and tried to follow the directions he'd downloaded from the Internet. At three places where his directions said to turn left, he faced "No Left Turn" signs. The one right turn he took led him into the parking lot of a commercial bakery. The smell of baking bread started him salivating, hammering home how long it had been since breakfast. Stomach grumbling but too impatient to stop and grab a snack from his food stash in the trunk (though he made a mental note to keep said stash on the passenger seat next time), Henry drove round and round, convinced he'd typed in the wrong zip code into the map website and pulled directions for the Excelsior Hotel on Bizarro world.

And now me am found, he thought.

Defeated, he turned into a gas station to ask for help only to find himself forced to swerve away at the last moment to dodge a neon-green, energy drink delivery truck careening out from the clearly marked entrance. With a shocked yelp and squealing tires, Henry barreled down a one-way service road that, fortuitously, brought him to the Excelsior. Less fortuitously, the hotel stood on the opposite side of an eight-foot chain link fence topped with barbed wire. Henry took some small comfort, however, in verifying the Excelsior's existence on this earth. A mere forty-five minutes later, he found his way round to the proper entrance and rolled into the parking lot. He pulled into a spot, placed his head on the steering wheel, and exuded a long sigh of relief. It quickly became a strangled half-scream of terror when a bone-jarring jolt shook Henry's car with a resounding thud and a metal-and-plastic crunch. Henry's head scraped against the wheel and bumped the windshield, his moment of peace shattered.

Rubbing his aching forehead, Henry spotted the silver bulk of an oversized pickup truck in his rearview. He exited his car and gaped at where the pickup, backing from the opposite spot, had caved his rear bumper and trunk into a deep, V-shape.

Now in all fairness, the pickup's driver — a squat, bald man in a tweed sports coat and a Tom Baker scarf coiled around his neck — apologized and took the blame, which, considering Henry's vehicle had been stopped during the collision, would've been difficult to dodge. They traded insurance information, and after Henry told the man why he was at AstonishingCon, he even promised to come by and buy a copy of Henry's book. He seemed so contrite that, as he drove away — a sparkly "I Vacation on Gallifrey" sticker glittering on his back bumper — Henry felt his luck might be improving. It was a warm, fuzzy feeling… that deserted him when he discovered the dent in his trunk had jammed it irretrievably shut.

Henry tugged; it didn't budge.

Henry tugged harder; his car creaked and rocked on its suspension.

Henry hauled back, and gave his trunk the hardest, most damning roundhouse kick a purple belt since age thirteen could muster. Missing his target, his sneaker scraped the car surface and kept going. Momentum yanked Henry off balance. He over-compensated, flailed his arms, and plunged to a hard landing on his rear. The impact rattled his teeth. His lack of padding only emphasized his mother's complaint that he didn't eat enough. Imagining cartoon stars and lightning bolts swirling around his bony butt, he conceded that on *this* she might be right. From the ground, the dent in his trunk resembled the warped grin of a robot clown about to razz him. A snarky Transformer. But Henry couldn't imagine any Transformer willing to disguise itself as a Saturn. Econotron and Compact Prime just didn't have the right ring to them.

Henry climbed to his feet and reminded himself not to sweat the small stuff.

"Um, this isn't the small stuff," he corrected himself.

With all his copies of *The Mercurial Hearts of the Stars*, his table-top poster and book display, his business cards, his food and drinks and clothes, and everything he else he needed for three days at

"The World's Most Astonishing Convention" all held hostage by a broken trunk lock, the argument seemed settled.

"Maybe," Henry muttered, "the Universe is saying I don't belong at AstonishingCon."

He could almost hear the Universe, VALIS-like, beaming him its advice: *You don't need this aggravation. Don't waste your time. What if you go to all this trouble, and they don't like your book? Go home. Binge-watch* Farscape *then take a nap. Monday morning, get up early and apply to law school. Make your mother happy. Live a prosperous and respectable life supporting her many grandchildren.*

Except the Universe sounded suspiciously like Henry's mother.

If she were talking to him through an electric fan.

And pausing every other sentence to chortle and snort.

Henry pressed a hand to his forehead to check for fever, felt cool skin, and decided he was cracking up. He put a positive spin on his mother's rude gesture and imagined her slamming the front door, only this time slamming it with a resounding thud on the wheedling voice of the Universe. The voice fell silent. Instantly Henry realized he could get into the trunk by folding down his back seat and dragging everything out that way. Twenty-nine awkward, sweaty minutes later, his boxes and gear stood stacked on a handcart, and Henry pushed his young life's work into the Excelsior Hotel.

Signs in the lobby led him to the Con registration table.

That, however, proved to be for people buying tickets to attend the Con. The volunteers there sent him to a third-floor room — which turned out to be the Programming Ops room, and the folks there sent Henry down one floor to what he learned was the Con Ops room. There a woman in a *Next Generation* Starfleet uniform with a plush parrot pinned to her shoulder and an eye patch over her left eye sent him back to the first floor and instructed him to follow a different hallway.

Feeling faint from low blood sugar and desperate to pee but afraid to get lost seeking the Men's Room, Henry obeyed. Several elevator stops and two tight squeezes later, he found the Promised Land.

The Dealers' Room.

Where a bearded man in a kilt and armed with what appeared to be an actual battle ax refused to let him in without an exhibitor badge. Equipped with more directions, Henry returned outside and made his way around back to the loading entrance. As he wheeled around the hotel perimeter, having searched for nearly an hour and now passing within fifteen feet of his wounded Saturn, Henry thought he heard the Universe snicker.

The laugh sounded so much like his mother's, it made his skin crawl.

He gritted his teeth and approached the vendor registration table.

A scrawled sign on the abandoned table read: "Back in 15 min."

Henry groaned, propped his cart by the open door, and peeked into the room.

Everywhere people worked arranging displays of books, DVDs, statues, artwork, games, clothing, weapons, jewelry, and more. Henry wondered which of the tables was his. In the far corner of the room, right by one of the main doors, an imposing man with a great silver beard sat, organizing stacks and stacks of books and comics on his table. Henry wondered if the man had written them all and how anyone could be so prolific. It had taken him two years to pen *The Mercurial Hearts of the Stars*, and after four months, he had written only two chapters of its sequel, *The Cold Love of Black Holes*.

Behind Henry, someone coughed.

Henry whirled to face a frowning woman built like a walking barrel. Letters emblazoned on her bright red T-shirt said: "AstonishingCon Vendor Wrangler."

"Help you?" she asked.

"Ah, yes, I'm here to debut my first novel, *The Mercurial Hearts of the Stars*." Henry tapped his stack of boxes then chuckled. "I hope I brought enough."

The vendor wrangler rolled her eyes. "I'm pretty sure you did. Name?"

Henry gave his name then waited while the woman flipped through a box of envelopes, starting with L. She came up empty then switched to the front and rolled through each envelope all the way to the last. She eyed Henry, and her lip twitched. Henry stepped back. The woman pulled a laptop from beneath the table and opened it.

Her fingers clacked the keys.

Cla-klick, cla-klick, cla-klick.

Pause. An exasperated huff.

Cla-klick, cla-klick, cla-klick.

"You sure you're registered? Dealers' room is sold out, you know."

"I'm sure." Henry unfolded a piece of paper from his pocket and showed the woman his confirmation number. "Here, look."

"Ohhh," the woman said, frowning.

"Um," Henry said. "There a problem?"

"A problem?" the woman said. "Why would there be a problem? You put a flaky artist in charge of all the Dealers' Room registrations and badge preparations, and you know what you get? You get the most beautiful badges ever to grace AstonishingCon." The woman, still typing with one hand, held up a badge where a colorful and lushly rendered alien landscape surrounded the white space left for a name. Rocks in the landscape spelled out "EXHIBITOR." "See? I got a hundred just like it. Only you tell me. What's missing?"

"Um," Henry said. "Aliens?"

The typing stopped.

"Was that a joke?" the vendor wrangler asked.

Henry guessed. "Yes?"

The woman's squint deepened, but then she smiled, and then she guffawed. "Aliens! Hah! He should've drawn them holding up name placards. That's what I'm missing: *names*. Our would-be Michael Whelan didn't put anyone's names on any of the badges." Still laughing, she dragged a boxy, wireless printer from under the table, switched it on, and ran out a label, which she peeled and stuck to a badge, covering half the art, before handing it to Henry.

"Table 36 1/2. Hang a right. Go all the way to the end."

"Thank you," Henry said. He looked at his badge, which read: Henri Lyn. "Oh, um, just one thing, this badge, my name is—."

"Henry, I like you. Let's keep it that way."

Henry said, "Sure, but, um—."

"Next," the woman called.

A man with an armload of light sabers, who seemed to have materialized out of empty air, stood right behind Henry. From the beads of sweat on his brow, his hunched posture, and the pleading look in his eyes, Henry guessed the light sabers were in fact rather heavy. He shoved his misprinted badge in his pocket, then wheeled his things into the room as the man crashed his weapons onto the table, eliciting a disgruntled growl from the "Vendor Wrangler."

Now Henry readily admitted he lacked expertise when it came to author appearances. He'd been to a convention or two and a few bookstore signings, and he thought he grasped the general idea. The author sat behind the table; the fans lined up to buy books. Win-win. At none of those events, however, had the author ever sat at a table tucked behind a three-foot diameter ceiling column. Nor was any author Henry had ever met flanked on one side by a twelve-foot banner for *Time Demons*, a homemade movie with the world's loudest trailer soundtrack, and on the other by a solid wall of tabletop strategy games stacked so high they blotted out the overhead lights, eclipsing Henry's table into perpetual twilight.

He double checked the number written on the Post-It stuck to the table.

36 1/2. No mistake.

At least there was a chair for him.

He wanted to ask for a better spot but changed his mind after realizing the Dealers' Room would open in fifteen minutes. Instead, he unloaded and stocked his table, stacking books on one side of the column and setting up his poster on the other. As he fussed trying to make his books as visible as possible, a loud voice across the room warned that the doors were opening to the public. Henry shoved all his boxes and bags under his table and took his place.

The doors opened.

Henry braced for the onslaught.

A man walked in, carrying a tray of sodas and a bag of Chinese take-out to one of the exhibitors. Next came a couple who walked straight over to the silver-bearded man across the room, picked up several of his books, and thumbed through them, smiling. Some kids raced each other to the bootleg DVD table, where they argued over the movie titles.

Then… no one.

Half an hour passed. A few more people trickled in, most leaving before they reached Henry's corner. The next half hour brought more of the same, as did the whole hour after that.

"What the hell?" Henry said. He approached the director of *Time Demons* next door and shouted, "Where is everybody?" The heavy metal soundtrack savaged his voice.

"I'm Al," the director said.

"Henry," Henry shouted. "I asked where everybody is."

"What?" Al said.

"Where is everybody?" Henry practically screamed.

"Oh, sure," Al said. "It's about time-traveling demons. They're demons who build a time machine to sneak out of Hell for a road trip so they can get back before the Devil knows they're gone."

Henry blinked, at a loss for words.

Al handed him a postcard of the *Time Demons* poster. Photoshopped devils raised sloshing beer mugs around what looked like a giant blender with an iPhone glued to the top welded onto the roof of a Cooper Mini. "Here, have a postcard."

Henry took it and said, "Could you turn that down?"

"What?"

"I said, could you turn that *down*?"

"Not sure yet," Al said. "We might have clowns in the sequel. Clowns are as creepy as demons, sure, but Time Clowns doesn't sizzle as a title. You know?"

Henry slunk back to his table. He considered asking the game dealer, but the man seemed entombed in his inventory, eyes peering out through a chink in the wall. So Henry rearranged his display, neatening his untouched stacks of books, business cards, and bookmarks, and the blank sign-up sheet for his mailing list. Another hour passed before a bespectacled, gray-haired man in a Green Lantern T-shirt approached the table. He reached for Henry's book but stopped short of picking it up. Henry stood, heart pounding.

"Hi," Henry said. "This is my first novel. Would you like to hear about it?"

The man yanked his hands back to his chest like a mortified house maid in a Hammer horror movie. "I don't have any money on me. This is my first walk-through. Like to see what's here. Gotta budget, you know. Just walking through, but I'll be back around," the man said. "Promise, I'll be baaaack."

With that he fled, borne away on the currents of the hard-rocking "Theme from *Time Demons.*"

By the nine o'clock close of the Dealers' Room, Henry had sold not a single book and given away only three bookmarks, and one of those to an eight-year-old who spit a wad of gum onto it, crumpled it up, and shoved it into his pocket. Al silenced the *Time Demons* trailer, and Henry's ears rang in the abrupt quiet. He thought he glimpsed the gaming dealer scuttle into a large box under his table and pull the lid closed after him, but he told himself he was only imagining it, loopy after a long day. Overhearing comments from the other vendors about how slow Fridays were with people still arriving at the Con, he hoped Saturday would be better. Time to check in to his room, grab a bite, then catch some sleep for what he expected would be a big tomorrow.

After forty-five minutes on line at the front desk, the hotel clerk informed him with an irritated smirk that he had no record of Henry's reservation. The Universe whispered in Henry's ear, urging him to take this as another sign. *Give up,* it told him. *Do something better with your life than waste it suffering one nuisance after another just to shill books to an indifferent public.* As tired and worn down as Henry was, if the voice of the Universe hadn't still sounded like his mother, he might've done exactly that. Instead he dug in, slapped his reservation confirmation e-mail on the counter, and demanded a room upgrade for his inconvenience. He didn't get the upgrade, but he did get the key to a room on the third floor, a last-minute cancellation.

Henry's rush of triumph proved short-lived.

Wedged between the elevators and ice machines and across the hall from the Con's main party room, Henry's room offered a veritable no-sleep zone. He didn't care. He carded the door open, dropped his luggage on the floor, and crashed on the bed. Tugging a pillow over his head as the "Theme from *Time Demons*" blared from the party, he prayed for sleep.

Things would be different, if only—like his Uncle Gao in the story—he could pray to the Monkey King to end all his woes. Later, he finally dozed off, mumbling, wishing for the Monkey King's help, repeating the words Gao claimed in his story to have used to summon him. After a while he slept. Beer-swilling demons on the prowl for premium weed and scantily clad sorority girls from every decade stalked his dreams.

The next morning, a good-sized crowd materialized in the Dealers' Room.

No one, though, stopped at Henry's table.

He stood out in front and offered them candy.

"Hi. Can I tell you about my new book?" Henry said. Or, "Hey. Would you like to see my first novel?" And sometimes, "Do you like good books?" or "Have some chocolate and check out my book."

Eye rolls. Head shakes. Blank stares. Scurrying feet. Promises to be back later. Even one giant sneeze. These were the responses he received.

Finally a man in a "Cthulhu Saves—For He Might Get Hungry Later" T-shirt picked up a copy, skimmed the back, then said, "Wow, I love stories about *stars*, man. Like when the *stars* are right. Or Star *Wars*, Star *Trek*, Star*gate*, *Battlestar Galactica*. Oh, look!" The man's eyes wandered to a display on the next aisle. "Autographed photos of Richard Hatch!" He shoved the book back at Henry and rushed off.

A woman in a *Firefly* uniform flipped through a copy then asked, "What's it about?"

"Space romance. It's about the princess of a star-spanning empire," Henry told her. "She becomes cut off from her people at the same time an alien invasion begins, and it's up to her to unite the frontier worlds and organize the defense."

"So it's like a political version of *Star Wars*?" the woman said.

"It's an adventure," Henry said. "There's romance and intrigue. Good guys, bad guys. Aliens. Assassins. Lots of danger. And strange technology and stuff."

"This princess, is she also a scientist? Or a medical doctor? Or a dominatrix?"

"Huh, what? No. She's good with technology. And she has mad people skills. People love and idolize her."

Shaking her head, the woman said, "And you thought she was worth writing a whole novel about? I guess at least you didn't publish it yourself." She glanced at the spine. "You didn't, did you?"

"What?"

"*Self*-publish."

"No," Henry said. "Loki's Library Press published it."

"Well, there you go."

The woman handed the book back and left Henry befuddled. And thirsty. But he knew if he drank another water he'd have to go the Men's Room, and he didn't want to leave and maybe miss a sale. He dropped into his chair and groaned. His hunger kicked in and he dug a granola bar out of his snack box, wishing instead for his mother's homemade dumplings and fried rice. He'd planned to buy food with the money he made from selling books, which left his restaurant budget at zero. The granola bar, pilfered from the pantry at home, stopped his stomach from grumbling, but it left his soul ravenous.

The "Theme from *Time Demons*" rolled through him for the umpteenth time, an earworm so potent he feared it had rewritten part of his DNA by now so that he would never stop hearing it. Al sold another DVD of his movie, emptying his third box of the weekend. Henry checked out the gaming vendor's table. People bought card packs, dice, and game boxes; they pushed money through the opening in the wall of games where the vendor's pasty fingers grasped it like the tendrils of a sea anemone curling around a clown fish. Henry wanted to pack up and go home. He stared at the far side of the room, where the silver-bearded man was selling yet another stack of books to a smiling reader. "Come on over and meet the author," he shouted, his voice somehow carrying through the *Time Demons* din. A small crowd gathered to listen to him.

In an alternate dimension, that's me and el beardo is over here high and dry, dancing with the Time Demons, Henry thought. *Ah, what the hell, the guy must be one hell of a writer to have so many readers. Good for him.*

By the Saturday close of the Dealers' Room, Henry had subconsciously taken to praying to the Monkey King under his breath, not realizing he was repeating his ancestor's words from his story. Two days and not a single sale. What kind of author was he?

Exactly, the Universe said, and Henry decided he'd left most of his marbles strewn on the Jersey Turnpike somewhere near the Clara Barton Rest Stop. *Can't you take a hint when the Universe hammers you over the head with one? If no one wants to read* The Mercurial Hearts of the Stars, *how many people do you think will want to read* The Cold Love of Black Holes? *Right! Less than nobody. You'd have more luck finding someone to pay you not to write it. Go be a lawyer. Lawyers write. They write legal briefs. Case summaries. Threatening letters. Good fun. Very creative. You don't need to languish behind this table to....*

"Oh, shut up," Henry said. "I paid for three days. I'm staying."

By Sunday, morning, though, he wished he hadn't.

Saturday night proved too painful for Henry to remember the next morning.

He recalled setting off in search of food, unable to force himself to choke down another granola bar and warm Pepsi from his food stash, and getting caught up with a cosplayer mob that carried him like driftwood on an ocean tide to a party. He knew he'd drunk booze because that's how one earned the megaton headache booming behind his eyes — and there were thirty-two (he counted) mini, single-serve liquor bottles scattered around his room. Except for the agony throbbing inside his skull, though, the over-imbibing didn't bother him as much as the rainbow-colored feathers littered everywhere. Or the furry Darth Vader costume in his bathtub. The take-out food packages seemed innocuous enough, but the two human teeth wedged into the remains of a cheeseburger unsettled him a touch. He checked; at least they weren't his. He had no idea what he had done that had required a sword, either, or why he'd woken up spooning a laundry bag full of women's underwear and leather corsets. There existed, Henry decided, a fairly good chance that the answers to these questions would prove worse than the mystery. So he decided to ignore them. He whispered a last wish to the Monkey King, then resigned himself to riding out the final hours of his first—and last—Con. The truth of his failure hit home while he sat at his table, head pounding, eyes squinting at a room empty of customers, except for three at the silver-bearded guy's table, where he promised to "dance like a monkey for a nickel," his voice again beating back the guitars roaring from the speakers beside Henry.

"You can go home anytime, you know," a voice said. "We're pretty much done here."

It sounded like his mother, like the Universe, like cars grinding through traffic and the ka-ching of money that landed in every-one's hand but his, like the chuckling, taunting disembodied voice that had heckled him since Friday—but at the same time, it sounded different. It sounded *present*. Henry looked up. The deep, sparkling eyes of Shiu Yin Hong—the Monkey King—gazed back at him. The Monkey King held a small ceramic bowl from which he ate something spicy and steaming. Mushrooms. Scallions. Beef. Cinnamon. Rice. Exactly like Henry's mother made. The aromas hit Henry's granola-choked appetite like an epinephrine injection to his taste buds.

"AstonishingCon broke my brain," Henry said. "Or I hit some heavy hallucinogens last night."

"Compared to what you got into last night, hallucinogens would've been tame." Shifting his gold and blue robes, the Monkey

King hitched himself up onto the corner of Henry's table, where he continued eating, smacking his lips. At a snap of his fingers, the "Theme from *Time Demons*" dimmed. "Why so surprised, Henry? How could I deny prayers from the descendants of the great Gao Chi Lin, who so accurately recorded how I created the Grand Canyon, a true marvel of the world? I've been with you since you left home."

"Not like a guardian angel, that's for sure."

"Weeellllll…." The Monkey King shrugged.

"Hey, wait," Henry said. "I didn't start praying for you until Friday night."

The Monkey King nodded. "Never said it was your prayers I answered."

The voice of the Universe. *Her* voice. His *mother's*.

"No!" Henry said.

"Yes!" the Monkey King said.

"My mother set you on me. Put you up to it all. The traffic! The accident! *Furry Darth Vader in my bathtub!* Making mischief. Driving me crazy. Trying to make me quit and go be a lawyer or a computer programmer."

"Excellent choices. Your mother will be very proud. Let's pack up and go."

Henry sat stunned, paralyzed. The Money King made his rice bowl vanish. A succulent orange took its place. He peeled and devoured it in moments, and the sweet, citrus scent filled the air, taunting Henry's shriveled stomach. Licking his fingers clean, the Monkey King bounced down from the table and began to gather Henry's things, but the simian deity jolted to a stop when a man's voice boomed from behind him.

"Excuse me," the man said. "What are *you* doing here?"

The Monkey King winked at Henry. "Only you can see me, Henry. He must be talking to you."

"No, I'm not," the man said. "I'm talking to Shiu Yin Hong. I see you just fine."

The Monkey King swiveled to face the silver-bearded writer from the table across the room.

"What are you doing here?" the man said.

"Packing up books," the Monkey King said.

"I can see that," the man said. "Why is the Monkey King at AstonishingCon?"

"I am helping my young friend along the path to success."

"Oh, really? Helping him give up and go home? Strangle his dreams in the crib? I heard what you told him on my way back from the Men's Room. I may be getting on in years, but I'm not deaf. Or dumb. His mother put you up to this. *His mother.* And you don't stop for one second to think what's right for him? What's best for Henry? What does he want? Some nutty old broad without a creative bone in her body says jump so you jump? What is wrong with you? I've heard of callous, fickle gods, but you're the Monkey King. You're a friend to poets and artists. You're supposed to *get it.* So I ask you again: What are you doing here?"

A smoky red glow swirled all around the Monkey King. He tripled in size, looming over the silver-bearded man, over the entire Dealers' Room, blotting it out, a menacing, cosmic primate only Henry and the other man perceived. "How dare you speak to a god in that tone," the Monkey King said. "Bad enough you see me when I don't want to be seen by you. Now you'll answer *my* question and tell me how that can be."

"I know you're a god. That's why I'm so amazed to see you here," the silver-bearded man said, staring up at the Monkey King. "And I can see you because I've written truthfully about you and helped grow your legend. I've brought you new fans on at least two continents and in all five boroughs of the great city of New York. And because gods rely on people's faith to exist, that part of you grown by my stories gives me awareness. I can see what others overlook."

The Monkey King *harrumphed* then shrank back to his normal size.

He rubbed his chin, frowned at the silver-bearded man, and tapped his paw in the same dismissive manner as Henry's mother. "I know you," he said. "Henderson, right?"

"That's right."

The Midnight

"Hmmm, I must confess, I do like what you've done with me."

"Well that just warms the cold cockles of my heart," Henderson said. "Now answer my question. *Please.*"

The Monkey King shrugged. "Eh, I make mischief and I go where I'm wanted. I'm not too picky about the outcome. His mother prayed to me, said her kid was going to taint the legacy of the great Gao Chi Lin with his purple prose, and she couldn't bear it."

The Monkey King tossed Henderson a copy of *The Mercurial Hearts of the Stars*. The author caught it then thumbed through the pages with interest, skimming a few lines.

"You write this?" he asked Henry.

Henry nodded.

"You want to write more?"

Again, Henry nodded, left speechless by confusion and his raging head pain.

"Let me tell you something." Henderson set the book down on the table. "You want to write, *write*. You want to be a lawyer or a computer programmer, go be a lawyer or a computer programmer. You want to be a fireman, go do that. No one's stopping you. But do it because it's what *you* want to do. Every second of every day, we all do exactly what we choose. No one's holding a gun to your head. No bolt out of the blue is going to strike you down. Every second. Of every day. It's your choice how you live. Don't let your mother browbeat you. And don't put up with this knucklehead's monkey business." Henderson glanced at the Monkey King. "Did you even read his book to see if he's any good? Or did you just take his mother's word?"

The Monkey King shrugged. "I was waiting for the movie."

"Listen, Henry," Henderson said. "If it wasn't for storytellers like us, the Monkey King wouldn't even exist. You want to do something, *do it*. But don't think it happens overnight. I've been at this a lot of years and, trust me, it takes time, patience, and stubborn perseverance—*and* talent. Now I gotta go sell a few more books so I don't embarrass myself when I turn over all my hard-earned cash to the missus back home, but you know what you have to do, don't you? I mean, I'm not telling you which one of those choices is the right one. You have to make that call for yourself, but you *know* the answer don't you?"

Henry nodded.

"Good," Henderson said. Then he glanced at the Money King, squatting on the corner of Henry's table, sipping spiced tea from a dainty porcelain cup. "You — I'll be seeing you again real soon, Shiu Yin Hong. You and me, we're gonna have more words."

The Monkey King only blew on his tea, sending wisps of steam across the edge of the cup. Henderson returned to his table.

The Monkey King sighed. "How about that blowhard? Who you going to listen to? Him or your mother?"

Henry shoved a copy of his book at the Monkey King, nearly unseating him from the table. "Who are you — or my mother — to say I'm no writer? You haven't even read my book."

The Monkey King took the book. Hesitantly, he opened it and skimmed the first page, making odd faces with his elongated monkey lips. Then he scowled and vanished in a puff of glowing red smoke.

"Hey," Henry shouted. "That's fifteen bucks!"

The Monkey King returned. "I'll pay you if I like it. Don't worry, I'm a fast reader," he said, then vanished again.

Henry slumped into his chair and let his head hang. As the adrenaline faded, the throb crept back into his skull. Despite his pain, he was glad he'd stuck out the weekend. Even if he was losing his mind, imagining conversations with silver-bearded authors and the Monkey King, it had helped him cross a bridge inside himself, one under siege by his mother for years. Now, calm prevailed. He did know the answer, the right choice. If it took years or a lifetime struggling, he would stick with it. How could he offer any less in honor of his Great-Great-Great Grand Uncle Gao, who'd suffered so much more than Henry to make his poems and stories? No sooner did the question cross his mind than the room seemed to brighten and a shadow fall away. Henry raised his eyes. The column blocking his table disappeared.

He had no time to indulge in wonder, though.

The diminutive Doctor Who fan who'd rear-ended his Saturn stood where the column had been, flipping through a copy of *The Mercurial Hearts of the Stars*.

"Been looking around for you all weekend," he said. "Glad I finally found you. This sounds great! Will you sign it for me?"

The man handed Henry the book and fifteen dollars. Henry autographed the book then thanked his very first customer. His first real reader. Or perhaps his second. The Monkey King read fast, after all, and who else could've altered reality to remove the column blocking Henry's table and obscuring his book from view. Maybe the Monkey King had placed it there in the first place, only to remove it after deeming Henry's book worthy. Whatever the answer, light poured in, and over the next two hours, others came. The man in the Green Lantern T-Shirt. The Richard Hatch fan. The woman in the *Firefly* uniform. And still others, many of whom had passed by Henry over the weekend, glanced his way as if they could almost see him but not quite. Now the veil had been lifted, and they found their way to his table. He felt happy greeting them, talking about his book. They listened to his sales pitch. They bought *The Mercurial Hearts of the Stars*. Henry sold one entire box of books before the Dealers' Room closed.

Exhausted but elated, Henry packed up to go home and wheeled his things outside.

While he was loading his car, Henderson drove by. He tapped the horn then slowed and rolled down his window.

"Hey, kid. See you next year?" he asked.

"Damn straight," Henry said.

"*Good.*"

Henderson tapped the horn a second time before rolling by. He turned toward someone in the passenger seat as he passed. Henry thought he glimpsed a flash of blue and gold fabric there, a tuft of monkey hair, a protruding simian lip. He thought he heard Henderson say, "Worked like a charm." Then before Henry could make sense of it, Henderson sped off to the highway and the next con down the road.

Afterword

Can you hear it?

Calling to us from the depths of a convention Dealers' Room or the pages of a pulpy novel or collection of short stories? That voice that beckons to us, tempting us to join it in the realms of wonder it knows so well. That voice whispering stories meant to be told and retold, read and reread until they take on a life of their own.

It is the voice that understands the subtle intricacies of storytelling. Whether they are stories that make you laugh, cry or, cringe, not one of them leaves you untouched.

Sometimes the voice is gentle and encouraging, coaxing you to listen. Other times the voice is gruff and curmudgeonly, impatient, not having time for your excuses, not understanding why you don't want to visit the big wide world of imagination.

To the authors who contributed to this anthology, that voice belongs to C.J. Henderson.

C.J. has touched every writer here in one way or another. He had a way of inspiring you, of making you better than you ever thought you could be. C.J. brought you into an unparalleled world of imagination. To some he was a collaborator, to others a teacher and mentor and, once he befriended you, he became your greatest cheerleader. He was continually creating opportunities for the writers in his circle. This collection may be one of the last of those but it will not be the last time we see him or the writers he has influenced in print.

C.J. once said that he usually had between fifty and one hundred projects in different stages of production. Some of those have seen published, but there are many more waiting to be released. With luck we will hear his voice for many years to come regaling us with new tales.

The editors had originally hoped to release this collection before C.J. passed but the universe decided otherwise. He did, however get a chance to see and give his input to most of the pieces presented here.

This was our way of honoring the man who gave so much through his writing and his friendship to us, the science fiction community, and the world. We have tried to do what C.J. would have wanted to celebrate his life, what he taught us to do.

We told stories.

Now go out and live, write, or tell a tale of your own.

It will make the big man smile.

Greg Schauer

Editor and Friend

John French -
What Stories He Knows

John L. French is familiar with crime and monsters. Having worked over thirty years as a crime scene investigator he has witnessed more than his share of what horrors one person can inflict on another. Working with patrol officers and detectives, John has been involved in putting many of these people behind bars for very long sentences.

In 1992 John began writing stories based on his training and experiences on the streets of one of the most dangerous cities in the country. His first story "Past Sins" was published in Hardboiled Magazine and was cited as one of the best Hardboiled stories of 1993. More crime fiction followed, appearing in Alfred Hitchcock's Mystery Magazine, the Fading Shadows magazines and in collections by Barnes and Noble. Association with writers like C.J. Henderson and James Chambers led him to try horror fiction and to a still growing fascination with zombies and other undead things. His first horror story "The Right Solution" appeared in Marietta Publishing's *Lin Carter's Anton Zarnak*. Other horror stories followed in anthologies such as *The Dead Walk* and *Dark Furies*, both published by Die Monster Die Books. John's first book was *The Devil of Harbor City*, a novel done in the old pulp style. This was followed by *Souls on Fire: the Chronicles of the Grey Monk* and *Past Sins: the Casebook of Matthew Grace*. John was also consulting editor for Chelsea House's *Criminal Investigation* series. His other books include *Here There Be Monsters*, *The Assassin's Ball* (Written with Patrick Thomas), *Paradise Denied*, and *The Nightmare Strikes*. John is the editor of *Bad Cop, No Donut*, *To Hell in a Fast Car*, *Mermaids 13*, and *With Great Power …*(with Greg Schauer).

John's collaborations with C. J. Henderson include stories in *Lai Wan: Tales of the Dreamwalker*, *Steam-Powered Love* and *Challenge of the Unknown*. John also edited *Challenge* and "interviewed" its host, Marv Richards.

One of these days John may get a website and a Facebook page. Until then you can email him at jfrenchfam@aol.com.

The Devil of Harbor City

John L. French

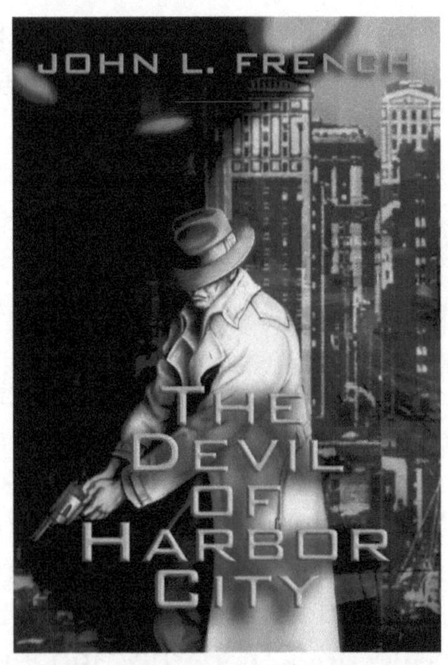

Dark Quest Books
ISBN: 978-1-937051-59-4 • **$14.95** • **208 pages**

It was a different time … A time when mob rule had replaced the Law. A time when Justice could be bought and sold. A time when the city was governed from the shadows. It was also a time when one man could make a difference. A man of courage and determination, a man willing to whatever it took in order to make things right. Frank Devlin could save the city. But at what cost? His life - or his soul?

Jean Rabe - *Star Lights*

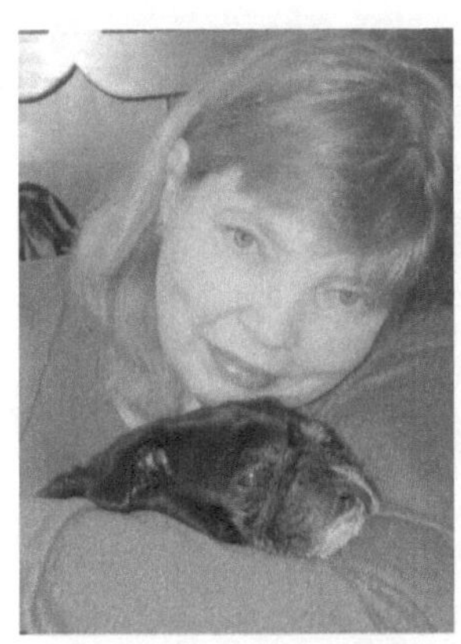

Jean Rabe has written thirty-three fantasy, science fiction, and adventure novels, and more than seventy short stories. When she's not writing—which isn't often—she's editing...more than 100 magazine issues and a couple dozen anthologies. Her genre writing includes military, urban fantasy, mystery, horror, Western, and contemporary.

She originally hales from Ottawa, Illinois, a smallish town divided by the Illinois River. It's where she learned how to play the clarinet, to treasure used book stores, to love football, and to appreciate the company of dogs. She attended Northern Illinois University, where she gained a Bachelor of Science degree in Journalism, with an emphasis on geography and geology. That's where she learned to play Dungeons & Dragons.

Her first full-time newspaper job was for the Quincy Herald-Whig in Quincy, IL. Her newspaper career took her to Evansville, IN, where she ran the Western Kentucky news bureau for Scripps Howard. She played still more role-playing games, helped run local game and science fiction conventions, befriended Timothy Zahn, exposed a corrupt county jailer, was shot at on a country road while covering an embezzlement story, and traipsed through flea markets held at an aging racetrack.

Tiring of reporting on the assorted acts of violence people commit on each other, she applied for a job at TSR, Inc. in Lake

Geneva, WI. TSR produced the Dungeons & Dragons game that she was still playing at the time. She interviewed one chilly February day for the position of RPGA Network Coordinator, and accepted the offer the following day. She worked for TSR nearly eight years, leaving to write fiction full time.

She's taught writing classes, run the Gen Con Writer's Symposium for seventeen years, has mentored authors, lectured at conventions, fused glass, played games, and tossed more tennis balls than she can possibly count to Duncan and Missy. She still appreciates the company of dogs.

The Love-Haight Case Files

Jean Rabe and Donald J. Bingle

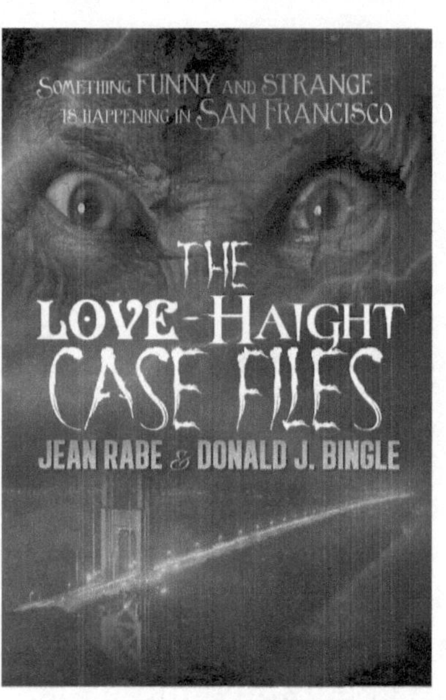

WordFire Press
ISBN: 978-1-61475-275-2 • Release Date: May 2015

San Francisco. Haight-Ashbury. It is midnight in the Summer of Love. Thomas Brock and Evelyn Love are attorneys who crusade for the rights of OTs—Other-Than-Humans. Their clients include ghosts, gargoyles, vampires, and things that have not yet been given names. The city's OT element is sometimes malevolent, sometimes misunderstood, and often discriminated against. Brock and Love represent them, whatever the case, whatever the species.

Magic hangs heavy in San Francisco, and danger and intrigue is as thick as the fog around the Golden Gate Bridge.

Patrick Thomas - *Henderson Rising*

With over a million words in print, **Patrick Thomas** keeps busy writing the fantasy humor series Murphy's Lore (which includes *Tales From Bulfinche's Pub, Fools' Day, Through The Drinking Glass, Shadow Of The Wolf, Redemption Road, Bartender Of The Gods, Nightcaps, Empty Graves* and *Startenders*) as well as the urban fantasy spin offs *Fairy With A Gun, Fairy Rides The Lightning, Dead To Rites, Rites of Passage,* and *Lore & Dysorder.*

His *Mystic Investigators* paranormal mystery series includes *Bullets & Brimstone* and *From The Shadows* (co-written with John L. French) as well as *Once More Upon A Time* and *Partners In Crime* (co-written with Diane Raetz). *Assassin's Ball* is his first traditional mystery, co-written with John L. French. He co-edited *New Blood* with Diane Raetz; *Hear Them Roar* with C.J. Henderson and was an editor for the magazines *Fantastic Stories of the Imagination* and *Pirate Writings.* His stories have been published in over three dozen magazines and more than fifty anthologies.

Patrick's humorous advice column *Dear Cthulhu* is approaching its ten-year anniversary and includes the collections *Have A Dark Day, Good Advice For Bad People,* and *Cthulhu Knows Best.*

Startenders

Patrick Thomas

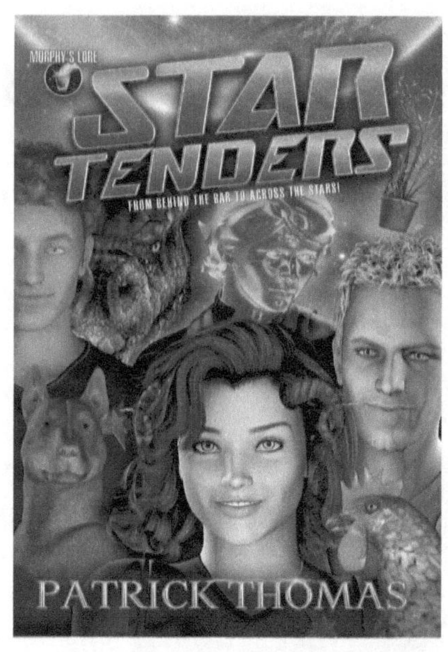

Padwolf Publishing
ISBN: 978-1-890096-58-8 • $15.00 • 240 pages

Sometime in the not so distant future...

John Murphy knows a thing or two about lending a helping hand. As a bartender at Bulfinche's Pub, he's helped the troubled for years. But now a mad sea god is going to sink New York City. Nobody's going to believe it, which means millions will die. But thanks to a time traveling message and a prophecy, leprechaun Paddy Moran has gathered legends together with brave men and women to form the Startenders, a group like no other the universe has ever seen. They have built a space station and a fleet of bar-ships and dedicated themselves to helping others. Murphy himself becomes the head honcho of the barship Fools' Glory and its crew of tricksters - Loki, Coyote, the daughter of Pan, a dragon demi-goddess, a golden melog and a sentient plant. But will even Murphy and the Startenders be enough to save the people of New York? Or prevent a genocide? Win a deadly game of spikeball? Help millions of aliens find their way home in time to spawn? Defend paradise? And most importantly, find the answer to the age old question - why did the chicken cross the galaxy?

Danielle Ackley-McPhail - *In the Dying Light*

Award-winning author **Danielle Ackley-McPhail** has worked both sides of the publishing industry for longer than she cares to admit. Currently, she is a project editor and promotions manager for Dark Quest Books and has started her own press, eSpec Books.

Her published works include five urban fantasy novels, *Yesterday's Dreams, Tomorrow's Memories, Today's Promise, The Halfling's Court:* and *The Redcaps' Queen: A Bad-Ass Faerie Tale*, and a young adult Steampunk novel, *Baba Ali and the Clockwork Djinn*, written with Day Al-Mohamed. She is also the author of the solo science fiction collection, *A Legacy of Stars*, the non-fiction writers' guide, *The Literary Handyman,* and is the senior editor of the *Bad-Ass Faeries* anthology series, *Dragon's Lure*, and *In an Iron Cage*. Her work is included in numerous other anthologies and collections.

She is a member of the Garden State Speculative Fiction Writers, the New Jersey Authors Network, and Broad Universe, a writer's organization focusing on promoting the works of women authors in the speculative genres.

When she isn't penning novels or other works of fiction she cooks, dabbles in costuming, and has stumbled upon a quite lucritive side business where she is known as The Hornie Lady, supplying fandom with handcrafted, one-of a kind costume horns.

Danielle lives in New Jersey with husband and fellow writer, Mike McPhail, mother-in-law Teresa, and three extremely spoiled cats. She can be found on LiveJournal (especbooks, damcphail or badassfaeries), Facebook (Danielle Ackley-McPhail), and Twitter (DMcPhail). To learn more visit www.especbooks.com, www.sid-hendaire.com, and www.badassfaeries.com.

Transcendence

Danielle Ackley-McPhail

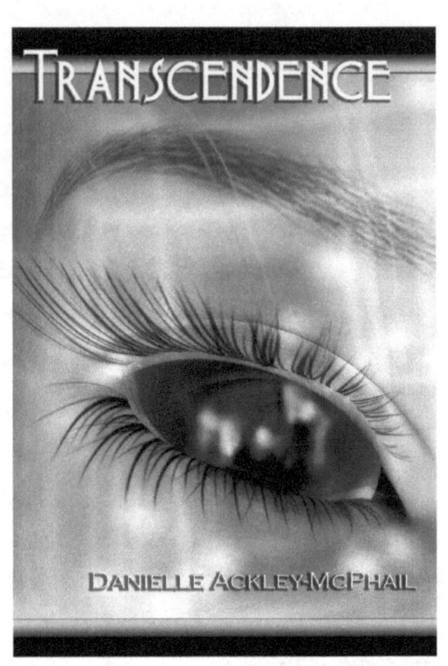

eSpec Books
ISBN: 978-1-942990-63-5 • $12.95 • 138 pages

What Will You Discover
Between the Darkness and the Light?

When the mortal coil wears thin and the great unknown draws nigh you might spy the narrow gap between the mystical and the mundane. You might even notice something's looking back.

Transcendence takes a hard look at humanity in nine tales of difficult choices, great rewards, and journeys beyond expectation.

The extraordinary awaits…
will you step beyond the bounds of commonplace existence?

Jeff Young - *Finder*

Jeff Young is a bookseller first and a writer second—although he wouldn't mind a reversal of fortune.

He received a Writers of the Future award for "Written in Light" which appears in the *Writers of the Future* v.26. He has contributed to the anthologies *By Any Means, Best Laid Plans, Dogs of War, In an Iron Cage, Fantastic Futures 13* and *Clockwork Chaos*. Jeff was also published in the magazines *Realms, Cemetery Moon, Trail of Indiscretion, Realms Beyond, Carbon14* and *Neuronet*. Jeff is an editor with Fortress Publishing for their *Drunken Comic Book Monkey* line as well as the anthology *TV Gods*. Fortress will also publish the forthcoming collection of his short fiction, *Diversiforms*.

He has led the Watch the Skies SF&F Reading Group of Harrisburg and Camp Hill for more than fourteen years. Jeff also is an instructor for the Step Back in Time class at Dreamwrights Youth and Family Theater. Step Back in Time prepares children to enjoy all aspects of Renaissance Faires by learning about dress, language, culture, history and more. Step Back in Time's eleventh year begins in July. Finally, Jeff is also the proprietor of the online eBay and Etsy shop Helm Haven, which produces Renaissance and Steampunk costume pieces.

TV Gods

edited by Jeff Young and Lee C. Hillman

Fortress Publishing Inc.
ISBN: 978-0-988799-12-7 • $16.00 • 300 pages

Your Favorite TV Shows
Done by the Gods Themselves!

The great pantheons of the world run amok through eighteen tales of wonder and hilarity. Discover how the Egyptian gods use night court for judging the souls of the dead. What will happen when an office of Greek gods gets downsized? Why are there Norse gods on a space ship? There are stooges building a world! Deities on game shows! Stay tuned for these shows and more!

"Reader discretion advised, these uniquely twisted tales may cause lack of sleep, sudden laughter and a change in perspective. You'll never watch TV the same way again."

—Maria V. Snyder,
author of *Shadow Study*

Leona Wisoker -
Shadow of the Infinite

Leona Wisoker started writing when she was eight. Her parents made the mistake of praising her work; friends and family alike have had to wade through piles of her writing ever since. This is, thankfully, not as tedious as it used to be (or so she is assured).

She writes speculative fiction, edits, teaches, blogs, and occasionally reviews books, music, and food items. She tends to choose reading material alphabetically rather than by subject or author, which has led her to read about alcohol, babies, coffee, dreams, echinacea, fungi, gumbo, Hades, and many other random subjects.

Leona's science-fantasy series, The Children of the Desert, is set in a world still struggling through a number of basic moral and developmental issues. The beliefs and strengths of each character are tested to the limit in the course of multiple intersecting story arcs. And, of course, there's a mysterious ancient race in the background that could destroy all life on earth if they get sufficiently annoyed. Anything less would just be boring. For more on the series, please visit: http://www.leonawisoker.com/series-one.

In 2013, she launched The Scribbling Lion, a business aimed at boosting the signal for highly talented small-press and indie writers, musicians, and artists. Find out more about TSL's mission and methods here: http://www.thescribblinglion.com

Leona Wisoker's short stories have appeared in *Futures: Fire to Fly, Andromeda Spaceways Inflight Magazine, Galactic Creatures,*

Sha'Da: Pawns, and more. Her first self-published novella, *Fallen City*, came out in 2014 through The Scribbling Lion.

She has lived in Florida, Connecticut, Oregon, New Hampshire, Las Vegas, Alaska, California, and Virginia; has experienced the alternate realities of Georgia, North Carolina, Arizona, New York, Long Island, and Italy; and believes that one day she will find an absolutely perfect cup of coffee.

Fallen City

Leona Wisoker

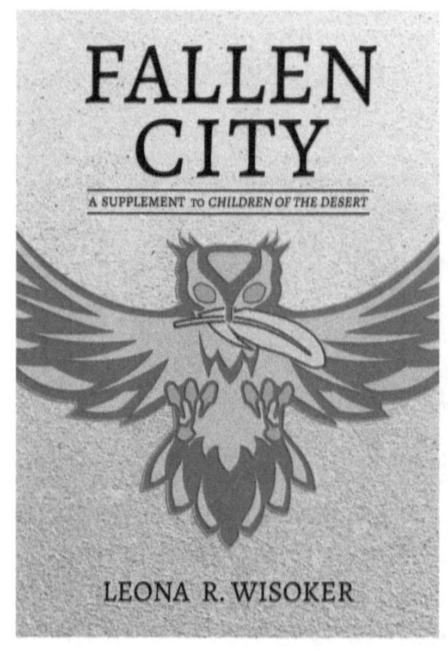

The Scribbling Lion, LLC
ISBN: 978-0-991317-11-0 • $6.00 • 78 pages

Deiq of Stass–a human-ha'rethe crossbreed called a ha'ra'ha–is worshiped as a demigod. He is immune to human laws, largely indifferent to human wants and needs. He seeks only to amuse himself–usually by stirring up trouble amongst the humans.

But even being all-powerful becomes boring, and spending so much time around the humans is changing his view on the insignificance of these frail, short-lived creatures. Ignoring the disapproval of his ha'rethe kin, Deiq pursues a new challenge: to breed a stronger, more telepathically sensitive line of humans that can bear his children without dying.

He should have stuck with being an arrogant demigod....

Robert M. Price - *Digging Up Doomsday*

Robert M. Price remains busy at his nefarious work and has put together several fiction collections now awaiting publication, mostly by Chaosium, Inc. These include *Secret Asia's Blackest Heart* featuring new Lovecraftian horrors set in Asia and Egypt; *Fumblers at the Latch*, a set of new Mythos tales; *The Mighty Warriors*, a collection of new Sword-&-Sorcery tales featuring well-known heroes like Elak of Atlantis, Imaru, Gonji, Thongor, and Oron; plus *The Yig Cycle*, *The Exham Cycle*, and *The Yog-Sothoth Cycle*.

Also on its way is Price's five-volume set featuring every bit of Lovecraft's fiction and some poetry, grouped thematically and with extensive introductory essays and individual story intros (Price's usual Chaosium format, this time applied to HPL's own fiction). *Azathoth and other Horrors* collects all the Cthulhu Mythos tales. *The Madness out of Time* brings together all of Lovecraft's "Revision Mythos" tales (stories dealing with his parallel mythology designed for his ghost-written tales). *Thaumaturgical Prodigies in the New-English Canaan* contains HPL's traditional "spectral" fiction set in England, New England, and Upstate New York. *Past the Gates of Deeper Slumber* features all the Dreamland and Dunsanian stories. Finally, *Pnakotic Fragments* collects the various juvenilia, marginalia, and the original drafts by Lovecraft's revision clients.

Invaders from the Black Lagoon is a forthcoming collection of brand new Lovecraftian fiction by Price. Contents include the title story, plus "Digging up Doomsday," "The Third Oath of Dagon," "Drums of the Devil Dance," "The Caliphate of Cthulhu," "This Is the Dawning," "The Shining Trapezohedron," and "The Gates of Baal." *Thongor in the City of the Gods* will collect all of Price's Thongor stories.

All these books are in process, but Price is still gathering material for more collections. *The Revision Mythos* offers stories featuring Rhan-Tegoth, Ghatanothoa, Nug and Yeb, Nigguratl-Yig, Gnoph-Keh, and Yig, Father of Serpents. *The Derleth Myuthos* features new stories of Ithaqua, Cthugha, Lloigor and Zhar, the *R'lyeh Text*, Laban Shrewsbury, etc.).

Cthulhu Detective

C.J. Henderson is widely regarded as the father of hardboiled occult detective fiction. His private eyes went head-to-head with the horrors of the Lovecraftian mindscape. Their weapons were fist cuffs, .45s, wise-cracks and harsh language. On occasions they got knocked down by a tentacle or two, but they got back up again, bruised and battered perhaps, and they kept on fighting. They were the first Cthulhu Detectives…

Cthulhu Detective features fiction from C.J. Henderson, Glynn Owen Barrass, David Conyers, Shane Jiraiya Cummings, Cody Goodfellow, David Kernot, William Meikle, Konstantine Paradias, Robert M. Price, Peter Rawlik, Brian M. Sammons, Ron Shiflet, and Jeffrey Thomas, with an introduction from Robert M. Price.

C.J. Henderson -
Sorrow

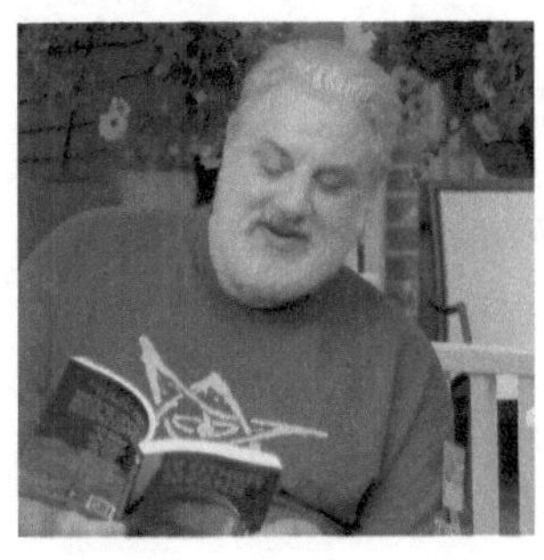

C.J. Henderson's early days were spent in the Midwest. The family moved around for the first few years of his life until finally settling in Western Pennsylvania, in Bridgeville (officially known by the sign at its entrance as, appropriately, the Town of Many Bridges), a small town outside of Pittsburgh. High school and college kept him in the general area, but shortly thereafter it was on to the big city, more specifically, New York City (officially known by the sign at its entrance as, appropriately, the Town That Doesn't Want You — Get the Hell Out!).

Because (a real fact coming up) out of all the people in America who actually make money from writing, only some 6% of them actually manage to support themselves entirely from such endeavors, C.J., like the grand majority of his peers, has had to come up with other ways to rake in the miscellaneous dollar or two. In his time, he has earned his keep and kicked around as a: movie house manager, waiter, drama coach, fast food jockey, interior painter, blackjack dealer, book reviewer, stockman, English teacher, roadie, advertising salesman, creative writing instructor, supernatural investigator, bank guard, storage coordinator, children's theater director, card shark, film critic, dishwasher, magazine editor, traffic manager, short-order cook, stand-up comic, interview & general article writer; toy salesman, camp counselor, movie booker, street mime, lounge lizard and as a senior editor of legal publications at Matthew Bender & Co., Inc. All too often, he still has to do such things. But, at least when one is writing film columns, the movies are free.

C.J. was married in all the typical manners to fashion designer Grace Tin Lo. They live in Brooklyn, NY, along with their daughter Erica, and everyone's cats, Tyco and Tiger.

Like every author, he managed his share of awards. His piece of the honors pie to date has been slim, but appreciated beyond measure. That list extends briefly to the following:

Awards: Best Newcomer of the Year (The Academy of Science Fiction, Fantasy, and Horror Motion Pictures), Best Short Fiction of 1997 (The Academy of Adventure Gaming Arts and Design), Year's Best Horror Honorable Mention (Ellen Datlow), 2007 Dream Realm Award for Best Anthology for Breach *the Hull*, 2009 EPIC Award for Best Anthology for *Bad-Ass Faeries: Just Plain Bad*, 2011 EPIC Award for Best Anthology for *Bad-Ass Faeries: In All Their Glory*.

James Chambers -
Every Second of Every Day

James Chambers writes tales of horror, crime, fantasy, and science fiction. He is the author of *The Engines of Sacrifice*, a collection of four Lovecraftian-inspired novellas published by Dark Regions Press which *Publisher's Weekly* described in a starred-review as "…chillingly evocative…." He is also the author of the short fiction collections *Resurrection House* (Dark Regions Press) and *The Midnight Hour: Saint Lawn Hill and Other Tales*, in collaboration with illustrator Jason Whitley as well as the dark, urban fantasy novella, *Three Chords of Chaos* and *The Dead Bear Witness* and *Tears of Blood*, volume one and two in his Corpse Fauna novella series.

His short stories have been published in the anthologies *The Avenger: Roaring Heart of the Crucible, Bad-Ass Faeries, Bad-Ass Faeries 2: Just Plain Bad, Bad-Ass Faeries 3: In All Their Glory, Bad-Ass Faeries 4: It's Elemental, Bad Cop No Donut, Barbarians at the Jumpgate, Breach the Hull, By Other Means, Chiral Mad 2, Clockwork Chaos, Crypto-Critters* (Volume 1 and 2), *Dark Furies, The Dead Walk, The Dead Walk Again, Deep Cuts, The Domino Lady: Sex as a Weapon, Dragon's Lure, Fantastic Futures 13, The Green Hornet Chronicles, Hardboiled Cthulhu, Hear Them Roar, Hellfire Lounge, In An Iron Cage, Lost Worlds of Space and Time* (Volume 1), *Mermaids 13, New Blood, No Longer Dreams, Shadows Over Main Street, Sick: An Anthology of Illness, So It Begins, The Spider: Extreme Prejudice, Qualia Nous, To Hell in a Fast Car, Truth or Dare, TV Gods, Walrus Tales, Weird Trails, Warfear,* and *With Great Power*; the chapbook *Mooncat Jack*; and the magazines *Bare Bone*, *Cthulhu Sex*, and *Allen K's Inhuman*.

His tale "A Wandering Blackness," one of two published in *Lin Carter's Doctor Anton Zarnak, Occult Detective*, received an honorable mention in *The Year's Best Fantasy and Horror, Sixteenth Annual Collection*.

He is a member of the Horror Writers Association, the current chair of its membership committee, and recipient of the 2012 Richard Laymon Award.

He lives in New York.

Three Chords of Chaos

James Chambers

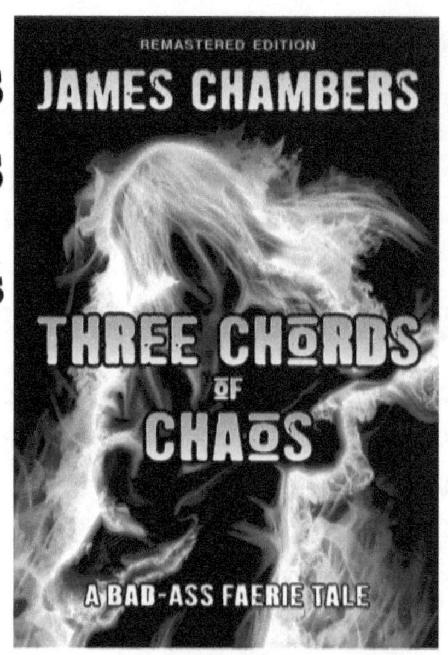

eSpec Books
ISBN: 978-1-949691-01-6 • $14.95 • 212 pages

Gorge never expected to discover such raw power, almost beyond his control, among the mortals who worship his music. Nor did he count on a mortal wizard to discover his secrets or turn the ancient weapons of the fae against him. Caught in a dangerous game of magic, music, and lies, Gorge must find the truth and uncover the source of his enemy's magic. Survival and love hang in the balance. And Gorge has only his music to protect him, only a song for any hope of salvation....

Greg Schauer - Editor

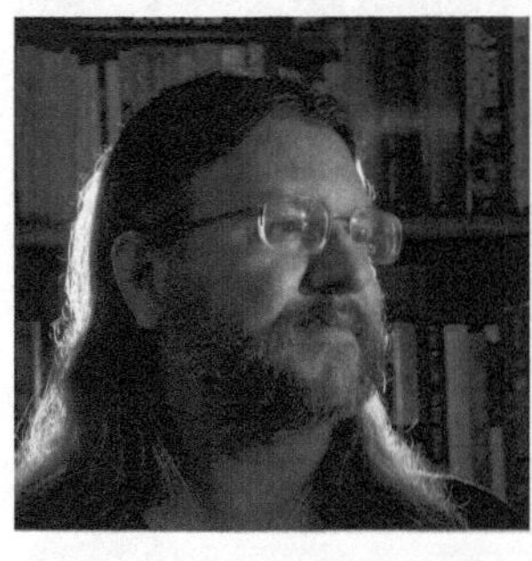 **Greg Schauer** has been a bookseller for over 33 years as the owner of Between Books in Claymont Delaware. He has also helped produce concerts by local and national bands at the Arden Gild Hall in Arden Delaware, one of the countries oldest continuously run secular utopian art colonies, for the past 10 years. He has previously worked on *Stories in Between:* the Between Books 30th anniversary anthology with W.H. Horner and Jeanne Benzel and *Steampowered Tales ofAwesomeness Vol 1* by Brian Thomas and Ray Witte and *With Great Power* with John L. French. He can be contacted at gschauer@betweenbooks.com

With Great Power

Edited by John L. French and Greg Schauer

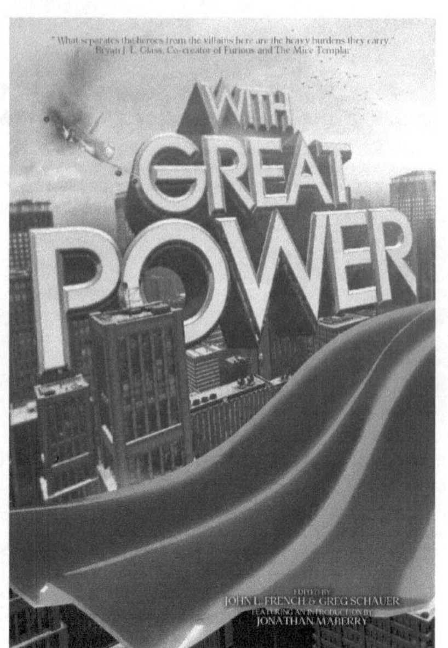

Dark Quest Books
ISBN: 978-1-937051-89-1 • $14.95 • 186 pages

Whether their powers spring from magic or technology, genetic mutation or exploding asteroids super powered beings have long captured our imaginations. Like modern day gods, they roam the earth displaying powers beyond mortal ken. Not always trusted by mere mortals, these beings do their best to mete out justice and save lives whenever possible. This thrilling collection is filled with heroic tales of daring, brought to you through the talents of: C.J. Henderson, Patrick Thomas, James Chambers, Gail Z. Martin, Hildy Silverman, Keith DiCandido, Bernie Mojzes and many more.

Jason Whitley - Illustrator

Possibly most remembered as the illustrator and co-creator of Wesley Craig Green's *Before Dawn*, **Jason Whitley** met CJ Henderson through mutual friend, James Chambers. Before introductions, Chambers warned Jason to hold onto his hat around CJ. CJ was a presence, to be sure, and a fast friend. CJ asked Jason to give Moonstone Publishing some sample pages for his Lei Wan comic book. Instead of black and white line art, Jason decided to make painted samples. He didn't get that job.

The Midnight Hour — Where all the secrets of the shadows are revealed... With James Chambers as writer, Whitley illustrates *The Midnight Hour*. Sea Urchins — The Moby Dick of webcomics

Jason's, and writer Scott Eckelaert's, comic strip, *Sea Urchins* follows the adventures of a family on board a huge houseboat lost on the oceans of the middle-earth-like planet, Terrasfumato. It was published by The Myrtle Beach Sun News from 2001-2005. Following that, it has been online at www.seaurchins.net. 2015 will mark the release of *Sea Urchins Book II: In the Shadow of The Sea Apes*. Book I was published in 2003 by Plan 9 Publishing and is now an eBook.

JASON WHITLEY has been published in *Negative Burn, The Book of Dark Wisdom, The Washington Post,* and *Inhuman*. His paintings have been displayed across the Carolinas and in Italy. By day, he is an educational multimedia developer at UNC-Chapel Hill.

The Official Roster of
The Society for the Preservation
of CJ Henderson

Adam Selby-Martin

Alexander "Guddha" Gudenau

Amanda Johnson

Amanda Waters

Amelia Smith

Andreas Gustafsson

Andrew Hatchell

Aussie Adventurer

Barb and Carl Kesner

Ben "Damocles Thread" Walker

Bodge Inglee-Richards

Brenda Cooper

Brendan Lonehawk

Bruce Press

Catherine Gross-Colten

Cathy Franchett

Cato Vandrare

Chris Quinn

Christian Steudtner

Christopher Northern

Chuck Parker

Cliff Winnig

Danielle Ackley-McPhail

David Zurek

Debbie Ronca

Don Corcoran

Donald J. Bingle

Drew J Cass

D-Rock

Duncan Dog

E. Alban

Elizabeth Howe

Ellen Gensel

Emily Lavin Leverett
eric priehs
Evaristo Ramos, Jr.
Furry Senpai
Gail Z. Martin
Gavran
Grant Klein
Greg Schauer
Guilded Age
James Chambers
Jason Russell
Jeff Young
Jen Thurman
Jenna Bird
Jim
Joe Murphy
Joeseph Simon
John "Shadowcat" Ickes
John Green
John Idlor
Jonathan Maberry
Joshua Hair
Joshua Ziegler
Kelli Neier
Kelly Farmer
Kyle Cassidy
Larry "Lordlnyc" Nelson
Laura A. Burns
Leshia-Aimée Doucet
Linda Pierce
Louise Löwenspets
Lynn Kramer
Maggie Allen
Marc Thorner
Margaret S. McGraw
Margaret St. John

Mark A. Schmidt
Mark Knapp Jr
Mark Lukens
Mary F Province
Matilda L. Madden, Ph.D
Mendel Schmiedekamp
Meredith Peruzzi
Michael Carson
Mike McPhail
Mike Spring
Missy Katano
Mr.& Mrs. Gregory Schwartz
Mystik Waboose
Nathan Duby
Nick Monteleone
Nicole Schwartz
Patrick Thomas
Pepita Hogg-Sonnenberg
Quintin Peterson
Rachel Marie Province
Ray Spitz
Rene Tang
Rob Balder
Rodney Romasanta
Sabrina Piazza
Sally Novak Janin
Scott A. Johnson
Scott Elson
Scott Goodell
Scott Johnson
Shervyn
Silence in the Library Publishing
Stacey Helton McConnell
Steven Tudor
Susan Glenn
Susan Pflug

thatraja
The Bailey's
The Dannenbaums
Thomas J. Talamini
Tina England
Tom Bither
Tom Carpenter
Tony Finan
V. Ayala
Vic Polites
Vicki Johnson-Steger
Wanda Beers
Wibble Nut
Will
Zan Rosin

Thank you all for your support.